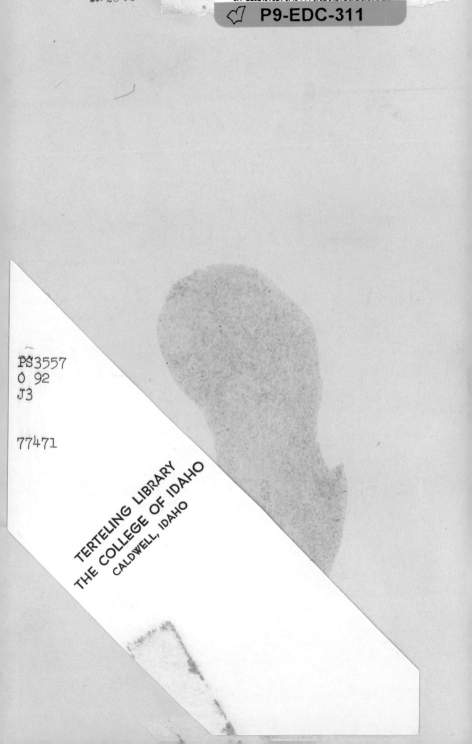

Also by Robert Gover

One Hundred Dollar Misunderstanding
Here Goes Kitten, *a sequel*
The Maniac Responsible
Poorboy at the Party
The Portable Walter, *an anthology*

J C
saves

by
ROBERT
GOVER

TRIDENT PRESS
NEW YORK

To Beverly Kay Mitchell and Odessa Levi

J C
saves

They'd been rioting in city after city across the nation, but not here. "Don't Let It Happen Here"— this was a motto both the city and the county were combined on. We'd joined forces to amass a tremendous effort. We'd enlarged both our police forces, given the firemen riot training, spent thousands for special riot equipment, and we'd alerted the National Guard. We'd done everything we could think of to prevent it, you see, so when it came we were beautifully prepared.

Okay, here's the scene: It's Saturday night and my wife and I have just finished dinner. It's our first weekend in the new beach house and all day she's been in the foulest of her foul moods, and now Junior is screaming for his dinner. In an attempt to tune them both out, I turn up the volume of the TV, and the next thing you know Junior's screaming is harmonizing with the televised screaming of sirens.

And here it is! Here at last! This violence in the

streets we'd worked so hard to prevent. Patrol cars, fire engines, ambulances, whole platoons of peace officers marching straight up Center Avenue in riot formation as our very own Negroes attempt to shatter our community image. All captured for time immemorial by our alert TV newsmen in their rented helicopter, swooping in and hovering low for classic shots of the action.

Which I was especially happy to see. One of my duties is to keep the gentlemen of the media prepared for such an eventuality as this, and here they were getting some absolutely marvelous footage, bringing the viewer right into the action. You could almost hear the thud as police batons were introduced to the heads of that unruly rabble.

But of course I couldn't just sit here and watch it on TV. At the next break for a commercial I grabbed my jacket and moved out with a vigor reminiscent of my Air Force days.

I had no idea my wife would misunderstand. Our marriage isn't what it should be, I'll admit, and all day long it was grouse about this and carp about that and nag nag nag. Naturally it was a relief to get out of there —I mean to be called out by professional duty. How did I know what it was destined to get me into?

I got a Jaguar XK-E now. It's the right symbolic statement at this point in my career—speed and arrogance —and, bet your bottom dollar on it, baby, I really laid her out on the Seashore Expressway. One hand on the radio dial fishing for fresh news reports, bombing along between ninety and a hundred. Slowed down at the Pennypacker Memorial Bridge just long enough to feed the automated toll collector, then ripped through Downtown and—would you believe?—I made it to the Mourn River Bridge in just under thirty minutes.

Here's where the action is, on the far side of the

Mourn River. A roadblock, a lineup of our combined peacekeeping forces. The riot helmets and special shotguns we'd purchased only last month now put to good use. Crowds of Negroes are being prodded into paddy wagons, and beyond that the clear reports from side arms, tommy guns, rifles, tear gas bomb-throwers, sirens—the instruments of law and order in a beautifully co-ordinated effort.

Virtual busloads of rioters pass me, going the other way. Off to a cozy little campsite we've prepared out in the sticks. And there won't be all that folderol about their civil rights or legal rights—I mean this is an emergency, so there just isn't *time* for the niceties.

Well, the boys on the roadblock are under the command of my good friend and associate Captain Hood, and he's been on the lookout for me. Because now that it's happening, our new duty is clearly indicated: to pinpoint the source of this virtual uprising. To unearth the incitement that caused this insurrection by fanning the flames of imagined discontent. Because the criminal elements who loosed this violence against these people must be found and punished. So Hood hops in my Jag and we're off for a tour of the territory.

It's all going strictly according to plan—that's plain to see. The men are doing their jobs with a detachment and efficiency that is truly magnificent to behold. Oh, the Bleeding Hearts will have a *good* cry over this. We're using live ammunition and the orders are Shoot to Kill. Yes, the breakdown in law and order is clearly evident in this riot-torn sector of the city. Plus reports of sniper fire. Persistent rumors, says Hood, of sniper fire, indicating that anarchy is just around the corner—that's why our guys are forced to use fire power.

Naturally there are bound to be a few casualties. It's all part of teaching them a lesson. A quick show of force

11

—that's our pattern of control. The overriding fact is, we're showing them how. I mean how willful destruction of private property can be nipped in the bud.

Skipping on, for the moment, to the final body count, we lost only one. A fireman in a tragic incident. He somehow got in the way of a speeding ambulance which was evacuating some policemen who'd been wounded by ricocheting bullets. Making it an even baker's dozen, thirteen deaths. But for publication— two. We don't like to frighten.

Unfortunately, things were beginning to quiet down by this time. I missed the climax. I was expecting it to happen *next* Saturday night, you see. That's why I'd been lolling around at the beach, trying out my new beach house. While Hood had been trying to call me since Friday evening—trying to call my town house.

But, no use crying over spilt milk. I'm in time for the mopping-up operations, and that's something. Besides, we've got our informational function to work on now.

Newsmen are being held at bay tonight, but they'll soon be swarming all over us wanting to know who, what, where, when and why. So we have some important decisions to make, the captain and I, for we don't want our stories to conflict. The news industry depends on us.

All right then, according to a certain-certain very secret contact the County has with this ghetto, the hot-spot is the Paradise Hotel, a hangout for all sorts of local vice. Dope pushers, prostitutes, black nationalists and other underworld types. So it's off to the Paradise we go.

We cruise down Center Avenue slowly, a very dark and eerie canyon now. The Power Company's had the wisdom and foresight to shut off electricity to this entire sector. Besides which all the streetlights have been shot out. The sidewalks are littered with overturned garbage cans and broken glass, and all the windows in all the stores are smashed—with one of our guys standing guard at each and every one.

Later it was determined that our tactics proved too much for those would-be looters. Our firemen stayed a jump ahead of the arsonists and most of the loss suffered by local merchants was due to water. Our nip-it-in-the-bud strategy worked beautifully.

Okay, so much for Center Avenue. Now up ahead, framed in the headlights and spotlights of a dozen or more patrol cars is the Paradise itself. And what a sight it is! Seven stories of eloquent evidence. I mean if anybody needs further proof of how violent some of our Negro elements are, here it is. Not a windowpane left in this whole building. Why it looks like something out of a World War II movie.

And as we pause here in front of the Paradise, Captain Hood expresses the conjecture that those black nationalist hatemongers are not likely to return to *this* place, not for a long, long time. And both of us philosophize a bit about their disregard for the private property and rights of other minorities. This hotel belongs to Sam Levenstein and you know how bigoted those certain violent elements are. That should explain the terrible havoc that was wreaked upon this fine establishment. I mean Sam's physical plant, his building. It was even rumored that one of them tossed a Molotov cocktail off the roof of this place.

But everything's under control here now, so we move on for a tour of the surrounding neighborhood. If, says Captain Hood—and here I quote directly——"if one of those jungle bunnies even thinks of burning or looting, he'll get his head blown off." End quote.

I can't let him get away with that. I chide him for

saying it in a perfectly untactful way, "jungle bunnies." I tell him, sure everything's relative—but. And I remind him that the *in* phrase is "violent elements." As Public Relations Officer of Hook County, I'm concerned about such things.

But who can blame the captain for being a bit disturbed? One glance around at all this destruction and any simpleton can see that all it does is defer the American dream of racial equality, so it's obviously Communist-inspired.

The important thing is not to panic. We've contained them in distant lands across the vast Pacific. There's no reason why we can't keep them under control here at home.

But I've let myself get sidetracked into morality. Let's get back to the objective facts. We're digging the scene, the captain and I. Awed by the sheer overpowering significance of it, this momentous event in the history of Hook County, and we're chatting about it quietly and in understatements such as, "Get on the horn to the meatwagon, tell those nellies where this garbage is at." Which is insiders' talk for, "There's one of them now, lying in the gutter. Put in a call on the radio-telephone to the ambulance division and have some attendant take it away."

But the streets are pretty clean. We only spotted two bodies. And the only action I got in on during that tour was when one of them ran out of his house, waving his arms and shouting obscenities at us. Just standing there in his doorway, shaking his fist and using some of the foulest language you can imagine.

All right then, Hood took out his service revolver and emptied it. That Negro's lucky he didn't break our baker's dozen and become body number fourteen. But Hood was shooting above and to either side of him.

Which did the trick—he ducked and disappeared into his house in a hurry, and so ended that little incident.

It could have been a lot worse, because we have two sound trucks making the rounds, telling them—I mean giving them clear warning to stay inside for their own safety. And that daddio was not only outside, but he was profaning a peace officer into the bargain—a peace officer with shoot-to-kill orders.

Well, other than that, our observation tour was somewhat dull and uneventful. About half an hour later I dropped Hood off back at the roadblock and I was about to head home to wifey and baby when. . . .

Let me put it this way. This insurrection was—no, strike that. This *riot* was such a climactic moment in our local history, and I am, you know, a maker of that history. And, well, I decided that one more look-see wouldn't hurt my function as a history-maker.

So I went back down Center again and when I got to the Paradise I cut left and went over to the street that rims the old railroad bed, and along that street.

Well! Guess where this takes me. To a deadend that turns up onto the street I have such a clear memory of. From six years ago, back when I was a college sophomore and decided one Friday night to take a look inside a Negro house of prostitution. A very forbidding street, this one. Lined on one side by that row of filthy old condemned clapboard shacks, which modern civic reform is soon to remove with the help of aid for urban renewal.

The point is, one's first impulse is to avoid this street, to make a U-turn and head back the way one came. All sorts of sinister things have happened to people on this street, my own misadventure being mild by comparison. So I did think twice before turning onto it.

I should have thought more than twice. Because the

moment I made the turn, my carlights picked up a hump. I mean, here was this hump lying in the gutter, and how could I have known it was destined to embroil me? That it was to force my role in this uprising across that hard line separating professional duty from personal involvement?

Us workin girls hangin out in the Paradize waitin on the police raid. Rescue Me playin on the jukebox. My themesong.

Yeah, cause I's flatout broke an down in the mind. Else I'd be on the phone t'my most mellow tricks tryin t'get one a them t'keep me for the weekend.

But what's the use. Nary a one gonna come over here t'fetch me. Not t'night. Cops all over thick as flies on a slopbucket, an they ain't lettin none a us go over there. Wolfie tried t'carry a couple a his broads over but they got turned back at the bridge.

This whole Saterdy night goin straight down the drain behind all that heat. Gonna have t'hit somebody jes t'eat.

Let's see who can I hit? There's Big Dot. I wonder can I touch her and I jes about t'ax her when she points a finger right back at me an yells, Hey girl, look out! Yonder come you a whuppin.

An I turns jes in time t'catch his fist upside my head. Knock me clean off the bar stool, right bam t'the floor.

Sonny, my ole man. Done strode in off the street an got up behind me.

But I's already on my feets again. Gots t'show him I ain't afraid. Gots to, else he ain't never gonna let up on me.

Get my feets unner me an I give a rush, put a fist in his belly hard's I can do it.

Never feels it. He's a Mahstah t'night. Liffs me up an throws me backwards, *wham*—I'm skiddin over the floor dustin this hotel with the ass a my dress. My secon' best catchin dress an I jes got it back from the cleaners t'day.

Well I'm up again, gonna use my heel on him this time, but security guard name Moze got him by the arms. Everybody pilin up around t'see it, girls jammin in between us. Moze say t'Sonny, Okay now, what's goin on here?

An Sonny tell 'em, You see what that bitz done? She think she's Mohamid Alley or somethin—runned up and hit me in the belly. That woman's tryin t'kill somebody.

She-it. Moze knows better. Knows I been trying t'cut my ole man loose behind him shootin up all my money. So I tells my side. Moze, you get that em-ef outa here fore I really does try t'kill him. Beat me outa every cent I made last night. Sneaked in my room after I done flat-back all Friday night, took it all an turned it inta shit.

Moze say, Look like you ain't wanted here, Sonny. You gonna leave? Or does I got t'give you a helpin hand out that door?

Don't give Son a chance t'answer. Turns him toward the door and *shoves*. He's half way out fore he knows it. Then he turn back an lays a spook eye on me, like sayin next time he see me out on the street he gonna sure enuff put me on the kickass express.

He been tryin t'have me crossed—till he found out mine's is to strong for it, so now he taken t'tryin t'beat on me. Pityful, that's all he is. Pityful.

Had six girls once, an now he ain't got a one. All he got now is the needle. On the hard stuff and goin out fast.

Somebody gonna finance him out, it ain't gonna be me. I ain't no weak sister, I's a strong-*strong* broad an I tole him over and over if they's one thing *no* girl needs in this life it's some deadend hype turnin all her flatbackin money inta shit.

Hey lookahere, the truth t'tell is, I tried. Oh yeah I did. I tried every which a way t'bring him back off. But the harder I tried the worser it got. Time was Son only took a skingraft once a week, a little trip t'dreamsville. But now he mainline commuttin t'nodsville twice a day. Got a habit like the nashional budjit.

I'm the last a his broads t'cut him loose, cause I thunk I was strong enough t'rescue him back. Humph. Now I needs a rescue.

Well he's gone now an I'm back at the bar again. Bartender set me out a house brandy, water back, an I'm tellin them other hoes, What good's a man like that gonna do? Polices pick you up and him skiddin around on shit—what good's he gonna be? Baby, with a man like that you gonna end up trickin fuzz jes t'stay on this side a the bars.

Gonna get me a new boyfriend, turn him out myself. Break him in the way I wants him. Lissen heah, I might even fetch me my most mellowest trick an turn him out, an I ever hear a him near that needle—mainline or skingraft either one—I'm gonna whup ass to a fare-thee-well.

19

Tell them other hoes that an we gets t'jerkin over takin some mellow white trick an turnin him out. That's jes talk—onlyest whiteman I ever had t'cross over, polices took him away for a crazy.

Yeah, they keeps the lid on pretty tight. Lookahere what brung on all this heat t'night. Other day some cop name Henry, he tole some teenage boy t'stop, halt. Ole Henry been warm for this boy some time now, sees him crossin the street an yells halt-halt. But that boy be damned if he gonna halt right in the middle a the street an maybe get runned down, so he kep crossin. Cop pulls out his gun an shoots, kills him.

An that's how come the other teenage boys went t'throwin rocks an bottles an whatnot, droppin 'em down on that cop. An that's how come all the fuzz is pilin up outside here t'night, fixin t'raid—man, them mothahs puts the Mafia to shame.

Dam, I don't know why they gots t'pick *this* Saterdy night t'do they thing, but they sure enuff here. Soon's somebody say *boo* at 'em, they gonna be doin they main number.

Look outside this hotel an there they go, four to a car, all wearin spacehats an holdin up rifles.

Wind-up toys, deadly mothahfuggin wind-up toys. An t'night they bees all winded up t'bust heads for a certain.

You ever had the cops t'spook you like that? Man, it's enough t'put the magic words in a preacher's mouth. Sure do got us workin girls hissin. Ready t'scratch each others t'bits. How everybody gets when they ain't no money comin in.

New girl, Jane, she fresh up from Alabama an still funky—she ain't got no age card, can't buy herself a drink t'nurse cause the bartender ain't takin no chances t'night.

An Olive, she's bullbitchin t'night. Got a hardon for brand new Jane. Been sittin cross the way lickin her lips an now she climbin off her stool an here she come rappin. Hey Baby, what's happenin? You looks some kinda seditty, off by yo'self like this. Lissen heh, I got somethin up in my room I'd like t'show you.

Jane don't know which way t'turn. Bashful, Olive gettin in her wig like this.

Sure does wanna party with Jane, Olive. An when she can't get her upstairs alone, she holler out t'everybody, Hey let's all go up my room, get high an freak off. What're we hangin round down here for? Ain't no mens gonna show t'night, no way.

Figure she gonna put follow-me powder on Jane like that. But no—Jane say she ain't goin t'no party, not unless Olive dredge up some mens t'pay for it.

Well Olive get t'coaxin, handlin Jane's dress an all, an pretty soon she jes plain give up her mojo an bingo! Second fight.

Jane lays a scratch down Olive's face an them two bitzes takes t'the floor, yowlin like alleycats. Rest a us broads all scrunchin up t'see it.

Olive the bigger a the two. An that scratch got her nasty. Way she be, if she can't get *in* it, she gonna sure enuff beat *on* it.

Hey but Olive rappin on a scrapper this time. Jane givin her tooth for claw. Both wigs gone an false fingernails flyin—man, they's out t'clean house with each other's nappy haids.

Till Moze run over. Scoops up Olive an lays her belly over a stool. Say, *Now* what?

One girl yells, Them two holes fell in luv, that's all.

Moze say, Oh yeah? This here one don't fall off that luv an ack like a lady she gonna get a floatout.

Jane come through the better a the two. Olive got

that scratch, an she gets up walkin with a crinch in her leg. An yellin—Where's my teef? Where's my teef? Lemme go, I gotta find my teef!

New teeth, set her ole man jes done paid for. They's layin off unnerneath another stool. Somebody pick 'em up and give 'em t'the bartender an he run water on 'em.

Then, right when Olive stickin her teeth back in an everbody settlin down again—out front a this hotel, them wind-up toy warewolves is gettin it on. *Rat-a-tat-tat.*

Holes scatter like corn. Forget the elevator an up them steps in a dusty ole Western, everbody talkin james bond, divin for the rooms.

They out there steady rat-a-tat-tattin so you can't hardly hear nothin else. Musta knowed jes when I gots t'my room too, them em-efs, cause no sooner'n I'm in the door, place fills up with flyin lead. Winda glass breakin all over the floor, plaster blatterin down on my head—ooh-wee, ole whitie's really in his bag t'night.

Been through my share a police raids, but never a one like this. Big Charlie can't starve us out so he set them warewolves tryin t'kill us. Sprayin bullets around like hailstones. An t'morra—doncha know it?—they gonna have it on the radio an tee vee that we *hates* 'em.

Whitie so hyped on shootin an killin, bomb-droppin an the like, he needs that shit worse'n my ole man needs his.

Lay on the floor till they point them guns on the next room, then I go scrabbelin outa my room. Hallway fulla girls. Cussin, cryin, beatin on the walls and belly-rubbin the floor.

An you wanna know who's the coolest bitz in the whole mess? Jane. Sittin a-gin the wall rollin a reefer.

I squats down an I puckers up right beside her. An

when she done rollin, she allows me t'fire up. Um-mm, a little taste sure do go good, time like this.

Well we's passin the smoke an lissenin t'the shootin outside, an here come a whole lotta sireens. A whole singin group a sireens, all wailin from every which a way.

Somebody yells out, Dig the blue-eyed soul music.

An jes when I's feelin better from that smoke an wonderin where can I get a pill for the night—all of a certain, who's that pokin his konk inta this hallway? My ole man! Got a hankerchief tied round his head an a tire iron in his hand, my very own blood in his eye.

Don't think twice about it. Grab my shoes an I'm on my way. Barefootin down the fire escape with that hype poundin along behind. Cut across the lobby inta the showroom, through there an out the back door inta the alley an the firstest car I see I dives unner it.

Lord-*dee*. What a *mess*. Police out gunnin for anybody's blackass an Sonny out after mine's. Ain't even got time t'wonder which is worse—that em-ef with his tire iron upside my wig or ole johnlaw's free ride t'the city morg.

Can only handle one at a time an Sonny's first in line—here he come out the door. Looks up an down the alley, and he take off trottin downways, and that's his mistake.

My mistake is crawlin out from unner that car too quick. Was gonna run back inside the hotel, but he seen me. An here he come.

Take off! Don't know where I'm goin but I'm sure enuff speedin. Out the end a the alley, cross the street an over Mary Johnson's gardin patch, down her alley, cross another street, an this street got no copcars on it so I'm beatin barefeets on it straight down the middle.

I know a lotta girls woulda turned to an took a whuppin steada this, but not me. I got my own rep t'perteck. Sonny out t'cut me so's I can't make it alone without him, an I's out t'keep my face jes like it is an show all them hozes they don't mess me up. Not this girl, an specially no hype.

Good thing he is a hype—slows him down. He was his ole self, he'd a caught me in a hurry. Now if I can stay a slip ahead, I can hide out in them bandid houses —that's where I'm headin.

Runned all the way t'the railroad an down that street, up the dirt alley t'the back a the bandid houses, an I throwed my shoes up through the winda a one, an I give a holler.

Ole Mother Mary, she in there. Reach a big arm down an pulls me up, an I no sooner gets my ass over the winda sill than he's here. Wheezin an gaggin an sick as a dog.

Got his hands on the sill, pullin himself up. Mother Mary takes up her stick, wops on his fingers. Falls back in the yard, but that don't stop him. Back he come an she steady woppin away on his fingers with her stick.

She about ready t'try her stick on his head, but all of a certain them warewolves is here. Out fronta these bandid houses shootin up *this* street.

Everybody on the floor, bullets zing zang zappin through, splinters flyin, dust fallin. Till they moves on t'the place nex door.

Stirred up so much dust in here I clean forget my ole man. Coughin an sputterin in this empty-empty room fulla all these real down peoples, an here come that em-ef. Again! Got his leg over the sill fore I get my ass a-goin. He's in through that winda for a stone certain

24

now, nobody there t'even slow him down. So sick he don't hardly know what's goin on.

Onlyest way for me is out the front door an hope the polices ain't lookin when I do it. Poke my head out for a quick look—*hey!* Somethin land on my back, *floomp,* an I cut outa there like a scared jackrabbit.

Thunk it was him gettin at me, but it weren't. One a them ole womens in there, she laid her army coat on me. Get-away present.

I hit the street jes in time t'see the copcar's red tail turn to the avenue. Whew! Head the other way an I'm all set t'scamper round that corner an find another place—*whoops!* Oh no I ain't!

More carlights. Somebody turnin onta this street.

Dive for the drainditch is all I can do. No time t'think it over. Plop down there an pull that coat over me head t'toe, and I *die.*

All right then, let's have a look at this hump. It appeared to be nothing more than an old overcoat someone had chucked out. The only really curious thing about it was how far it stuck up.

But that's enough, I decided. This is no time to let myself get carried away by curiosity. I was going past that hump, was actually cruising right by it when . . . well, I *saw* something.

Was it a *foot*? Is it possible that somebody's under that old overcoat?

So I changed my mind. Decided I'd better check it out. Jammed on the brakes and threw her into reverse and backed down for a second look. I shuddered at the thought that I was on top of discovering a corpse.

Then, suddenly, with the whole thing clearly visible in my headlights, an amazing thing happened: The hump rose. I mean it just lifted up out of the gutter and here were two eyes gleaming at me, glowing like the eyes of a frightened animal caught crossing a highway.

Well, being adventurous to a fault, here was a phenomenon I could not resist. This risen hump drew me out of my car. I moved in for a closer look. Even forgot to take the revolver out of my glove compartment, just got out and—

But now the hump rose higher. The next thing you know, here's a girl. Standing right up in front of me, holding this overcoat over her head. She's Negro—of course—and she's saying something, but the sight of her has chilled me, I'm frozen in my tracks.

What's she trying to say? Is she pleading, begging?

Then she drops the overcoat to her shoulders and now I can see her clearly—an icing of shock on a cake of surprise, because you'll never guess who I've just come face to face with. Kitten!

Yes, it was her, all right. With the headlights of my car full on her there's no question about it. Here is a female from my past, as unforgettable as the memory of that late great giant of civic reform, Herman Penny-packer.

I kept telling myself it wasn't possible, this just couldn't be. But she was jabbering away a mile a minute and there was no mistaking that voice.

I was stunned. It was like being in a strange city and meeting someone you *know* cannot possibly *be* there. I mean I'd been expecting to hear *of* her. The last I knew she was on her way up in show biz and I knew deep down that someday, somewhere, she'd turn up again. But what in the world is she doing here? In this ghetto. During this virtual insurrection. And what's she trying to say? Begging me—asking me not to harm her.

Harm her! Why would I harm her? Doesn't she

recognize me? If I hadn't been so stunned, I'd have picked her up, overcoat and all, and loaded her into my car, for my overwhelming urge was to *save* her.

Which, under the circumstances, would have been most unpolitic. I mean imagine trying to explain it to the boys on roadblock duty, a bundle like this in your car.

Well, I was on the verge of saying something like, Kitten, what are *you* doing here?—when out of the corner of my eye I became aware of movement. Back in the dark shadows. I turned to it just in time, because coming at me like out of the rotten wood of the nearest shack is a sinister figure—a man, and he's got a weapon, a club it looks like, and he's poised to leap at me like a wild animal.

Did I run? Baby, you'd better believe it. In that Jag and back up that hill like a jet. I'm not about to let curiosity crack my head open.

Well, the sight of her had shattered my professional objectivity. Yes, I'll have to admit, I was confused. Badly confused. You see, I knew what was required of me—that I report her whereabouts to the police, her and whoever my would-be attacker was, and let them handle it. But I was so shaken, so numbed, that I forgot all about reporting it. I just drove and kept driving, right through the roadblock with hardly a goodbye, and on toward the seashore in a trance.

My mind was like a movie showing quick reruns from the past. Her pixie grin six years ago when I first met her in one of those houses on that street. That sardonic smirk three years ago when the late and famous Mr. Pennypacker and myself ran into her as a singing sensation in the Fish Pond. The very same night, as fate would have it, of Mr. Pennypacker's mysterious disappearance and death.

28

Put yourself in my place and maybe you'll understand how shocked I was. It was like coming face to face with a dreadful memory. As if time didn't exist and the past three years hadn't happened.

No wonder I drove home in such a trance. All I can remember is some sort of lost, lost feeling. Wheeling down the very familiar Seashore Expressway—the Pennypacker Seashore Expressway—overcome by this weird sensation, these moments of not being sure where in the world I am. It's like I'd been drugged, doped and dropped onto some totally foreign landscape, and I had to struggle desperately to get my bearings, my sense of *where* I am and *who* I am.

And the shock was still with me when I reached my beach house. I just barely remember how terribly upset Barbara was. She was nearly hysterical, screaming invectives at me—but it all seemed to be happening to someone else. All I did was sit in the living room, only vaguely aware of her going back and forth, carrying things out to the car.

The next thing I know, she's yelling for me to come. Lock up the beach house and get in the car or she'll drive off and leave me here. Just like I left her, she screams at me. Which is when I managed to shout: "Go ahead! Leave!"

Which she then refused to do. Came back inside and began pushing me bodily out the door, down the steps, into the car. And away we went with her at the wheel of my Jag, J. C. Junior sitting on my lap bawling his little lungs out—all the way home.

Where, to make a long story short, I wound up in the dog house. She plunked the baby into his crib and tossed a sheet, pillow and blanket on the livingroom couch, then she went into the bedroom and slammed the door.

She didn't have to *put* me out. Not tonight. I'd have *chosen* the livingroom couch, if she'd given me half a chance. Because it certainly had me in a very peculiar state of mind, this thing of going to that race riot on perfectly legitimate business and suddenly coming face to face with someone who . . . well, anyone familiar with my previous written documents will bear me out—I have every reason to be shocked.

I was awake for a long time, trying to find a way to absorb the shock. To relate it to the rest of my life. Because I kept getting this frightening feeling of being caught up in some horrible dream I couldn't quite separate from my real life. It was like I would wake up in a moment to find that I'm not really who and what I thought I was.

Did you ever have such a feeling? Let me put it this way: Imagine you just learned you're part Negro. Not that it shows. Oh no. The only way you know is, your very own sister gives birth to a baby with Negroid features. Kinky hair, dark brown eyes, flat nose, cheekbones just so. And suppose this sister is married to a Swede. I mean a Swede from Sweden, from a pedigreed family background with absolutely no chance for Negro blood to have infiltrated his family tree. And suppose this baby looks, in many respects, just like this Swede. Okay, it's your very own sister's baby—right? And how much African blood can a pedigreed Swede have? So it's got to be your sister. Which means that you, too, are . . . how can I say it? Not pure!

Just a hypothetical situation, mind you. Just a way of conveying how I felt. I want that firmly understood. But the point is, ask yourself how *you'd* feel. What would you *think?* I'll bet you'd be pretty darned mixed up, right?

Well, you can take that hypothetical situation—

purely hypothetical—as an example of how I was feeling. But *why*, you might well ask. After all, encountering Kitten during that race riot isn't all that earthshaking, is it? I'm still the same good old J. C. Holland. I could pass for a men's magazine fashion model, and it's what's up front that counts. So *why*—why should I be plagued with these weird sensations of being somehow lost or misplaced!

And the truth is, I can't say.

Scared? Lookahere, I'm so scared I'm chasin my life through my head. Yeah, like it's doing a fast get-away an I'm rushin t'catch up.

Gotta be whitie in that car. Nobody else allowed out. An that whitie burnin them carlights on me. Can feel it clear in unner this coat. Liable t'step out an blow my head fulla lead. Carry me off t'the morg, pile me on top a the rest of 'em, rezistin arrest.

Then all of a certain that car moves on. Slides right on by me an I's about t'breathe again—but, URCH! Stops short an backs up.

I'da made a hole in that street if i coulda. Now I *knows* this Mahstahrace mothahfuggah got eyes for me.

Lay still a minute an I say t'myself, Hey Momma, you gonna go out cowerin like a whimpering dog? Or is you gonna rise up an look this devil in the eye and die shoutin magic words at him?

Got risin up in mind. Then I hear the car door open.

Peep out, and here he comes, moving right in on me.

Well now I ain't got magic word number one. Ain't nothin on in momma's mouth but prayers—I'm putting the whole deal straight t'god an allah both.

Time this whitie come t'where he standin right over me, I'm so fulla the oh-lord-geezuz-save-me shimmies, you'da thunk this coat's a gospel tent. Blinded by them carlights an my ears about t'split from the noise his iron gonna make when he puts lead in my head, and here's me, I'm gospel talkin the em-ef, I'm sayin, Oh lord-dee, plee-eee-eease. Please don't kill me mister. I ain't done nothin. Ain't never hurt you, have I? Please jes take me in or let me go, *please!*

Up so close I could reach out an touch him, an I sure am shoutin up his pantleg—jes's fast an hard's I can do it.

Then all of a certain, he's gone! Give a start, hop back in his car, screamin tires up the street in a whiz-bang hurry.

Hey Momma, you musta scared the hell outa that Mahstahrace! What I thunk—but oh no, weren't me. Lookahere right behind me—Sonny. That's who done the scarin. One hype's thing chasin off another.

I mean t'tell it like it is, seem nothin in life gonna stop this one. He got gettin up my ass in mind so bad he don't even know what else is happenin.

Fixin t'hop on an beat me like a drum. Wavin his tire iron around a little whirl, makin sounds like an evil wind. Callin me by the name I'm wearin now—Odessa, yoo-hoo Odessa. Come here, Odessa. Come t'dad-day, bay-ba. You ain't got nowhere left t'run, so come on back, bay-ba, and take what you got comin.

Jive mothahfuggah, if he weren't so sick, I'd sure enuff be gettin what he say I got comin. I seen him one time back when he was okay, seen him whump some

33

bitz's ass singsongin this way all the time he was doin it.

But that was the ole Sonny. New one's staggerin for a fix an them staggers is all I needs t'cut cross his path, up the street a few steps an in.

House next t'the one I broke in at. Up them circle-stairs three at a time, that fix-headed tire iron clumpin along behind, all the way up the five stories t'where they got the ladder t'the roof.

Ole Mister Rather at the top a that ladder. He sees what's happinin an lets me up. Good thing he seen it, too, cause I ain't got breath left t'tell it.

He's cool, ole Rather. Blocks the way on Sonny, an he say down, Hey boy, what you want here?

Sonny say, Outa my way, ole man, an don't call me boy or I'll beat the both of ya.

You ain't beatin nobody, ole Rather say, an he reach down an bop Son's head.

That drops him down the ladder. Standin there rubbin his head an shoutin up em-efs.

Rather ain't sayin a word, jes waitin. Got his fist balled up and hangin down through the trapdoor.

Then, lookahere, Sonny swings on him with the tire iron. Yeah, rare back an let go, but ole man Rather grabs that iron on the backswing an now he's got it, an he hangin it down there, waitin for Sonny's nex move.

Here's Son, Now Mister Rather, sir, you get outa my way. Please, sir. This between me an my woman. She been askin for it an you know a man can't let a woman get away with that, you knows that, doncha, Mister Rather, sir.

Me, I holler down, Sonny you nacheral sack a twenty diffrent mothahfuggahs, I *ain't* your woman. No *way*.

I done cut you loose behind you shootin up all the cents an I ain't nobody's woman, no way in *life*.

But the sound a my voice puts him rushin up the ladder again, an all that gets him is his own tire iron upside his head.

Rubbin his head again, cussin, moanin. Says up, Hey ole man, *keep* outa my bizness.

Anybody up here's my bizness. What ole man Rather say. You git out *my* bizness. Go on back down there an hit the streets. Go on home t'you momma, boy.

An here's Sonny—he's howlin. You gonna put me out on them *streets?* For the cops t'*kill?* Me, you own black *brother?* Mothahfuggah, you the coldheartest nigger livin, you do a thing like that.

But that don't cut it neither. Rather say, Go on home, boy. You know where, an you knows how t'get there.

That's the truth. Sonny got a sweet little granny'll take him in any time, an he sure do know how t'sneak around the streets. Can turn a corner in a wink, hyped or hurtin.

But he sure do hate t'give up whuppin me. Stallin, tryin t'figure a way round that tire iron.

I better see can I hurry him along, so I say, Sonny you is cut loose now an you is gonna *stay* cut loose, an the onlyest way you gonna get up my ass is t'cut that aitch loose. Now you go on back and maybe one a the black nashional brothers'll help you cold-turkey, cause ain't nothin more I can do.

He say—an ooh, what a nasty way he say it—he growl it up. I ever do, bay-ba, I'm gonna tear yo' face t'*pieces.* Then he do this mean put-on, he say, *Is yo' hip t'face pieces, bay-ba?* Well get hip, yo' devil-catchin nigger bitz, cause that's gonna be yo' *thing*—when I'm alright again.

35

Turns away an starts down. A sorry-sorry sight. An I can't help thinkin it sure do grieve my heart how the downpeoples kick ass on each others. They say the buck-passin stops at the top. Well the ass-kicking oughta stop at the bottom, but it don't. Goes t'the bottom an keeps on in a circle, faster an harder. An I sure wish I knowed how t'make it quit.

Halfway down, Son leans over the rail an hollers up at me, Dammit woman, gimme a nickel! Only a nickel! Is five ones gonna hurt? All I need is five an I'll get straight, you know I will.

Pityful. All I can do is say, Sonny baby, I ain't got a *one*. You done took it *all*.

Makes me mad all over again when I think of it. Took over thirty dollahs an shot up, then them other hypes beat him for the rest of it, an now we's both broke, an the only thing he can think t'do is jump my ass like it's my fault.

I jes turn away. Can't stand t'see him like this, cryin an groanin, so pityful.

Lotta peoples up here on this rooftop. They all crowdin in, tryin t'find out what's goin on.

I cut through 'em an go over t'the edge, look down an wait t'see Sonny come out the door.

Cops still poppin away now an then. Sound truck cruisin around sayin, Stay inside for your own safety.

Ain't that some kinda shit? What jokers! Shootin clear through walls an tellin people t'stay inside—for *safety!* She-it.

Godam Mahstahrace spacehat mothahfuggahs, one a these times all the black folks in the whole world gonna get dam sick an tired a bein shot at, an we's gonna turn to an shoot back. Yeah, an then them sons a suburb holes is gonna have it comin back around at 'em.

Anyhow, pretty soon, out he come. Bumps along

close t'the houses an makes it t'the corner, an that's the last I see.

Some little girl got a hold a my skirt an she sayin, Hey lady, what's that man gonna do now? Where's he gonna go?

Oh god, ain't my heart bled enough for one night?

I pick her up an I say, He goin home t'his momma, he gonna be okay now.

An she looks at me and she say, I ain't got no momma. Can I go home wiff you?

Oh geezuz! I sure wish I could be as deadhearted as they say a hoe spose t'be. Behind everythin else t'night, this little child—it's like she reach clear inside and is beatin the daylights outa me, heart an soul. Anybody can see she got a powerful need for somebody t'take her in. An all these peoples up here, they ain't got nowhere t'take her in at—none of 'em.

But godamit, neither do I. Hotel room's all I got, an they wouldn't let her in the front door a that place.

Done the best I could for her. Wrap us both up in that big ole army coat an rock us back an forth, till she went t'sleep. Up here on this rooftop, outside in the cold night air with them em-efs down there steady pop pop poppin all night long, freakin off on gunsmoke.

Sunday, Barbara and I took the baby to church, as usual. We smiled and exchanged pleasantries with other members of the congregation, as usual. The rest of the day—I dealt with the press as never before.

It was certainly a relief to get back to the Courthouse on Monday. Of course the place was in an awful uproar, my own office especially. Calls and telegrams were pouring in, congratulating and damning us. Out-of-town newsmen all over, complaining about not being permitted to interview key officials.

It was Meet-the-Press day for George Washington Jones, the board's Negro member. Whose task it became to convey the gratitude felt by responsible members of our Negro community, you see.

Poor George. A Stokely Carmichael he isn't. They had him backed into one corner of my office with the TV lights roasting him, and when he tried to copy the cool style of the infamous Stokely, his image went to pieces.

Of course I did all I could to help his image, but he lacks swagger and cool. I mean George acts like he thinks the world's one big sauna bath. And by the time that interview was over, he was one big mass of jangled nerves and smeared makeup.

Meanwhile, outside my office door, the courthouse corridor resembled a toppled beehive. People milling around, trying to button-hole VIP's and give them an Everyman's solution to the Negro problem. (Put *our* man in the White House and then we can *buy* them? For home consumption?) Anyhow, one of our foremost citizens was delivering a lecture about how we should have rolled in the National Guard tanks, and when I stepped into the hall he asked me why we hadn't. I'd have a devil of a time trying to tell him, without injuring his dignity, that when you bring in the National Guard, you're practically inviting the international news corps, and there's no telling what *they* might do to our image. So I sidestepped the issue by saying that the important thing is this: it's *we* who run this community, not the rabble, and our peace-keeping forces did a magnificent job of putting this message across. It's just a matter of communications between power and people. Let's be realistic: We're on top, they're on the bottom, and we all love it that way. So when the Word fails as a community organ, we use nightsticks. And when nightsticks do not turn the trick, we are forced to define our relationship in bullets.

That's life. Naturally there were some arms twisted, some heads bowed and bloody, some painful prodding of "innocents," so to speak. And now that some of them are no longer among us, the Bleeding Hearts are having a field day. Holding a cry-in, boo-hooing about alleged police brutality. Well, it's a free country—let them cry. Because when all the bodies have been buried and all the eyes are cried dry, perhaps they will reflect upon what has transpired. And perhaps next time they won't be so quick to tempt us with raw demonstrations and displays of defiance.

You see, we're really a very civilized community and we absolutely *hate* to use force. I mean we're not lily-livered—some of our younger peace officers are Vietnam vets, the finest fighting men in the world. Put guns in their hands and give the command and they'll kill, no questions asked.

Vietnam certainly was a valuable experience, a great preparation for the kind of disturbances we're having here at home. I myself pulled duty there as an Air Force information officer, and it left me with a perspective on these things I couldn't have gotten any other way.

For instance, before every mission flown, our guys were given character guidance by the base chaplain, who stressed the fact that we were visitors from a nation that worships the Prince of Peace, and our main task was to win the hearts and minds of the Vietnamese people. Therefore we weren't to feel—*not ever to consider feeling* conscience-stricken or responsible or collectively guilty or some such, for the inevitable innocent victim, because each and every mission flown saved American lives and shortened the war.

We're really a very remarkable people, when you stop to think about it. I mean it's no secret any longer that we have our own home-grown brand of Commie-style agitators, stirring up violence in the streets and trying to disrupt our way of life. Yet once we stop them, you'll find the mainstream American perfectly willing to forgive and forget. We'll end up healing their wounded, feeding their hungry and searching for ways to employ them gainfully. That's *really* what the American dream's all about, baby.

Which reminds me. Speaking of dreams, it was later that same Monday that I had a most startling dream. Frankly, it's a dream of such a personal nature that I wouldn't think of disclosing it in this document—if it weren't for the fact of my pen-name. Because it masks and obscures the *real* me. J. C. are my actual initials— this bears repeating—but those initials are much too common, both in church and out, for anyone to trace them to the real me.

Okay, when I describe this dream, understand that I do so with impersonal distance and objectivity. Like the style of the editorial. The editorial *we,* it's called. And that's right up my alley, you know, because of the nature of my profession.

Well then, it's the wee hours of the night after that frantic Monday, and I'm having this startling dream— of making love. I mean I'm holding this woman's . . . how should I say it? . . . her seat in the palms of my hands and she's rolling and writhing with ecstasy beneath me and—

But that's as much as good taste permits. The thing is, it's *Kitten* I'm making love to. In this dream, you see, and it all seems so real, it's a wonder I didn't actually say something like, "Oh Kitten, I love you." Which would have brought down the house! Because the next thing I know, I feel pincurlers gouging my face, and I come out of this dream to find that it's my wife. Here I am on—I mean in bed with Barbara. I'd sleepwalked from the livingroom couch to the bedroom and crawled in.

Well, it'll give Barbara something to tell her psychiatrist on her next weekly visit. He's helping her achieve orgasm with ease and unself-consciousness. Which she certainly did that night.

As for myself, it was a bit disturbing, waking up from that dream that way. My wife sighed and rolled over and went back to sleep, but I got up and wandered around the house. Couldn't sleep the rest of the night. Went back to the livingroom and got a fire going in the fireplace and stayed with that fire till dawn. Just stared into the flames thinking . . . remembering . . . wondering.

Sure it was only a dream. But it seemed so *real*. Well, it actually *was* real. There I was experiencing Kitten as my wife. I mean my wife as Kitten.

Now I didn't take psychology at State U. for nothing—I know that dreams are supposed to be an expression of the subconscious mind—but that doesn't make it less mysterious, because I must have been half awake. Maybe I was hallucinating!

Anyhow, I spent the rest of the night remembering—and with such vivid clarity it was weird. I remembered the time I was with her in her apartment like it was only yesterday, not six years ago. And the time in the motel room with the late Herman Pennypacker, rest his soul. But most of all I remembered her face that night of the riot—wide-eyed, intense. And very meaningful, as if she were trying to tell me something, or remind me of something.

I guess it's just a leftover from the shock of discovering her as a hump in a race war. Nevertheless it's gotten to me, pricked my conscience, my American sympathies for the less fortunate. Well, I'm not just an idle dreamer, I'm a doer, so as dawn came on Tuesday, I vowed to do something.

And as fate would have it, it was Tuesday morning

42

that myself and certain privileged members of the Board, at a private meeting in Chairman Herskovitz's office, came to the conclusion that a little CIA-type activity was in order, and that I was the logical choice for the job. It began as a very hush-hush affair, you see, and I'm not sure how much of this background I'm free to divulge. However, I can say this: that the County pays a substantial fee to a certain-certain Negro who poses as a "Hate-Whitie" sort. A marvelous street-corner orator and source of info from inside the ghetto.

But a question arose that Tuesday morning—should we trust this Negro *totally?* At which point, I volunteered to do what I could to check out certain tidbits he'd passed on, because factual information is my province, after all.

And this dovetailed nicely with my own personal urge to see her again. It gave me a split-level mission, you see.

It was understood that I was to obtain my information by whatever means I could. All the inner circle cared about was having a finger on the feelings of the ghetto.

I got to work that very afternoon. Drove across the bridge, high over the little Mourn River, so polluted by wastes now, way down there in its narrow ravine. The roadblock was gone already, and that was a bit surprising. And highly visible is this fleet of wrecking equipment. Well, it's about time! That row of filthy old houses of prostitution has been condemned for years. Today, at last, the wrecking ball falls. Three houses at the lower end of the street are already piles of rubble.

I turned left off the bridge and cruised slowly down that street, the rubbish-filled vacant lot to my left and that condemned row to my right. The third house down from the avenue—that's where I first met her. Now its windows are gone and loose boards dangle from its front. The door's gone and the whole place stares back at you like a skull.

So I cruise on by it. Don't park till I'm near the work site. Dump trucks coming and going. Steam shovels scooping up piles of rubble—old bricks and rotten lumber—and dropping them into the beds of waiting trucks. Load after load lands with a resounding crash followed by a cloud of dust. Decades of accumulated decadence. Shiftlessness, laziness, shoddy operations. Sin, lust, greed.

The hours went by like minutes. Before I realized what time it was, the workmen were quitting for the day, shutting down their contractor's equipment, getting into cars, driving away.

And then I was alone. Staring at that row of dead skulls, the houses that remained. It was hard to realize that not so long ago these houses were alive with Negroes selling and Caucasians buying. College boys, too young to know better. And was it possible that I had once been one of them? It no longer *seemed* possible. Well, be that as it may, by the end of the week this whole block will be cleared and the site will be available for some creative business venture—buying and selling of a more wholesome nature.

I was ruminating about this when I happened to glance up at one of those condemned ruins and my eye picked up some hint of movement. Up there at the edge of the roof. Or was I only imagining things? Because no one is permitted in these old shacks, and who'd want to be up there anyhow? They're certified unsafe.

Ah, but then I *did* see something move. Up on top of the tallest of these houses. Yes, something or someone was up there, no question about it.

44

But what to do about it—that's another question, and I drove home in a quandary. Feeling far from satisfied with my accomplishments that afternoon. In fact, I was so *dis*satisfied that I resumed my search immediately after dinner. Left Barbara to cope with Junior by herself, ignored her snide remarks and returned to my mission. After all, there are some things about a man that his wife just doesn't have to know about—right? (And in my own case, there is *one* thing she'd better *never* find out. It caused me sleepless nights before Junior was born and almost wrecked my parents—but there's no need to go into all that.)

So . . . where was I? Oh yes, here I am back on that ill-famed street in the ghetto. Now it's very dark and silent here. Across the river the city is lively with colorful neon signs and rows of headlights on the Thruway, but here there is only a death-like stillness. And a sort of slow-motion threat in the air, like any moment your life can be consumed by this very atmosphere of danger and terror, and I certainly hope the inner circle appreciates what they've gotten me into here.

I mean this ghetto certainly is a tragedy. An American tragedy. These Negroes are your countrymen and mine, and I'd go to the ends of the earth to save them—their money's as good as anybody's. I only wish they'd do something to help themselves. Look what a mess they've made of their own neighborhood!

That's what I was thinking as I stood there leaning against the fender of my Jag, watching that rooftop where I'd seen movement this afternoon, and wondering what the chances are that she might return to this street tonight.

Which I guess were pretty slim, and even if she did return, it would be darned difficult to see her. No streetlights. The only illumination is from the city lights across the river—just enough to show the lines and contours, and the holes where doors and windows used to be.

And even if I do see evidence that a person or persons are illegally inhabiting one or more of these condemned places—what should I do about it?

But before I'd come to any decision, my persistence paid off. There! Movement! No question about it! Up there on top of the tallest house, there are *people* up there. This time I was sure of it, absolutely.

Well, I'd just turned to get back in my car and go for a little police assistance when I heard the shuffle of approaching feet. Coming down the street, outlined against the lights from the avenue, was a man. I stood my ground, and when he got closer I saw that he was a thin old fellow, a light-skinned Negro, practically as white as I am, you might say. The only way I knew him for a member of the other race was his flat nose and shuffling gait.

He walked right up to me and peered at me closely. A hollow-eyed old bum with a week's growth of gray whiskers, wearing the trousers of an old-style police uniform. Stripes down both pantlegs.

He gave me this close once-over, then he was off down the street again. Gone before I'd even thought of asking him if he knew a girl called Kitten.

Which I didn't have much time to regret, because here was someone else. This one was walking with that brisk-bouncy stride some of them affect, and even before he reached me he was talking to me.

(I'd taken precautions, naturally. The gun I keep in the glove compartment—it was now in my jacket pocket.)

But he seemed friendly enough. A bit nervous and over-anxious, perhaps, kind of jerky in his movements.

46

I decided to question him. Asked him straight out if he knew where I could find a girl called Kitten.

Oh sure, he replied. Plenty of girls, plenty of kittens.

He'd misunderstood, it seemed. No no, I persisted, I'm looking for a particular girl by the name of either Kitten or Gigi Abercrombie.

Well, he stopped twitching and mumbling, and now he regarded me thoughtfully. Then he turned on a line of chatter which, as nearly as I can reconstruct it, had to do with a recent run of counterfeit money. Because of the riot, he said, there is all this counterfeit money floating around and things in the ghetto are "up tight."

Then he broke into a virtual denunciation of all counterfeit money everywhere. He stomped his foot and shook his fist at the sky. He practically ranted and raved about this "big run on bad bills."

Finally I interrupted this harangue to say that my money was as good as his any day, and I was even willing to pay something to learn the whereabouts of the girl I was seeking.

Okay, he said in a more subdued tone, "Follow me!"

Follow *him!* I shuddered at the thought. I weighed my well-grounded fears against the importance of this mission, however, and duty won. I followed.

He led me into the doorless entrance of the tallest house, and that took some nerve. It was pitch black inside—till he flipped on a tiny pocket flashlight and held it over our heads. Then he said, in a very confidential tone, that because of all the worry over counterfeit money lately, I'd have to show a sample of *my* money. Said he needed this sample to show to a woman upstairs, then she would help me find this girl I was looking for because she knows everybody—but she won't trust me till she's seen my money.

All right then, I hauled out my money clip and was about to peel off a sample bill when—*poof*. He'd snatched the whole clip out of my hand, switched off his light and was telling me he'd be right back.

I was standing there in this pitch dark, feeling pretty silly, letting him get away with that. Then he turned on his light again, and he was going up this spiral stairway—I watched the tiny beam of his flashlight as he went up to the second floor.

Now he was speaking to someone up there. Or so it seemed. In a loud, firm voice, he said he had a "customer downstairs" and here was a sample of his money. There was a pause, then he said, "Okay, I'll send him up." And down the stairs he came again.

"Give me my money!" I demanded.

He told me everything was okay now and that I should go on upstairs and see the lady up there, because she had my money, and she would put me onto the girl I was looking for. I mean, one moment he's standing right in front of me telling me this and the next instant—nothing. He'd vanished! Don't ask me to explain it—when I reached out to grab him, he wasn't there.

I figured the only way he could have gone was out the front door, so I stuck my head out and called, "Hey! Give me back my money!"

But I was only talking to the deadly stillness of the street—there was no one outside. Maybe he's still inside this foyer, I thought. I lit a match. And keeping one hand in my pocket on the gun, I held this match up—but the foyer was empty too.

I'd been conned! Suckered! Robbed! How could I have been so stupid? And him—instead of making an honest dollar by helping me locate Kitten, he turns anti-social on me and exploits me ruthlessly.

(Now I realize there are good Negroes and bad Negroes and you can't generalize, but it's this sort of thing that puts a black stigma on their race. And one of these days, we'll have to really crack down on them. We just can't allow such crimes and violence in the streets. I'm not an extremist, but at the moment I'd gladly have lined him and his kind up against the nearest wall and machinegunned them down. Because this would be a better world without *them*—right?)

Well, as you can see, being robbed didn't do much for me. After all, my tolerance does have its limits. I was seething with all this—just standing in the doorway, looking up and down that street, fingering my revolver and seething. Should I call it quits for the night, leave, come back tomorrow?

Or, I wondered, should I screw up my courage and just march up those stairs and have a look-see?

Darned if I'll be a chicken-hearted loser! I'm going up there, I told myself. Let's find out what's going on here.

When you're faced with such a situation as this, you do one of two things—you run or you overcome. I overcame. I took a deep breath and went groping through the darkness toward that spiral stairway, found it, then slowly, carefully, I started up. Cussing myself every step of the way for not having had the foresight to bring along a flashlight.

On the second floor landing, I paused long enough to run my hands along the walls. I felt doors but they were all boarded up tight. Not that I really expected to find a door to a room and come upon that thief's alleged lady friend. I just wanted to satisfy myself that he'd really been talking to himself up here.

All right then, I leaned over the banister and peered up, and way up at the top I saw a skylight. Which was

49

all I needed to beef up my resolve. No matter what the risks were here (and, believe me, this place was like a haunted house—even the walls seemed to be whispering all sorts of sinister threats) . . . no matter what the risks, real or imaginary, I had to check it out.

On I went. To the third floor, then the fourth. One more flight and I'd reach the skylight.

Wow! What a nerve-wracking business. Assuming there are people up there, they are Negroes. And they are probably armed and possibly dangerous. Maybe it's the hideout of some black nationalist cult with a cache of gas bombs and all sorts of weapons. They might even gun me down just because of the color of my skin.

All this was going through my mind as I put my foot down gently on the first step to the fifth floor, and when I thought I heard the sound of other footsteps. . . . Well, put yourself in my place. It gave me such a jolt I turned and went smack into the nearest wall.

Where I stayed, pressed against this wall, long enough to calm down and collect my wits. And also to check my revolver. (The safety was still on. Good thing—I had enough trouble already.)

Well, then I took a few more deep breaths and started up again. Whatever I'd heard up there, those sounds had stopped. There was nothing but my own breathing now. And this very hairy feeling that I was being watched by a million eyes, every step of the way. And if turning back and going down hadn't seemed every bit as frightening as going on up, I'll have to admit I might have turned back.

Slowly, cautiously, I went on up to the fifth floor landing. Now I was right under this skylight, this opening onto the roof, and guess what I found here. A ladder! That's right, an old wooden ladder going up through this skylight.

Wait'll I tell the boys at the Courthouse about this, I thought, as I fingered this ladder's splintery legs and tested its strength—the first rung, then the second, the third and—

Zoom! The whole world reeled. Suddenly I was suspended over the five-story drop down the center of that spiral stairway. My insides were jelly! I thought for sure I was a goner! The victim of my own good intentions, here in this house of horrors on a perfectly legitimate split-level mission. Is this to be my fate? Am I to end up a greasy spot at the bottom of this condemned ghetto dwelling?

Then I looked up and saw an arm. A hand. Someone up there was holding the top of the ladder, tipping it backwards, trying to drop me off it.

Well, I hung on for dear life. Had my face pressed against it—could actually smell this ladder's wooden mixture of evil and rot. Expected any instant to find myself on my way to my Maker—down, down, down.

When I heard a voice ask, "What do you want?"

And I looked up into the face of about as ugly a looking gorilla as you could hope to find anywhere—and all I could see were the whites of his eyes. My throat was so dry I could hardly blurt it out: "I'm looking for a girl. A girl called Kitten."

Which caused this gorilla to lean down through the skylight and squint at me like he didn't believe I was *real.* Then he said something like, Did I mean to tell him I'd come all the way up here just to find a girl?

Fortunately, I had enough wit left to realize that he was as surprised by me as I was by him. I said, "That's right. Sometimes she goes by the alias Gigi Abercrombie."

He made a noise, something between a laugh and a snort. I talked on, telling him I'd met her six years ago in one of these houses and that three years ago she'd been a promising song stylist in a downtown nightclub.

Well, I suppose that to his mind this explanation of my being here did seem a bit . . . unusual. At any rate, he laughed. Long and loud. Then he said, "Man, you *can't* be the police!"

I assured him he was right about that, and then—as if someone had uttered a magic word—about a dozen more faces appeared. Now there was a whole host of Negroes looking down through the skylight at me. Then the first man brought the top of the ladder back to rest against the skylight and told me to come on up.

And here I was on this rooftop, surrounded by a virtual horde of them. Negroes of all descriptions— male and female, young and old. All I could do was stand there gawking, amazed by the incredibility of the whole mess. Blankets and bedrolls scattered thither and yon, and off by itself was a pup tent. Are they camping out up here? Why aren't they in their homes? Or do they live here? I mean, what are they *doing* here?

Well, J. C., I said to myself, just act like you're a Green Beret who has stumbled into some remote Vietnamese village. Play it straight and don't blow your cool.

Ah, but they were as curious about me as I was about them. They were bombarding me with questions. Why was I here? What did I want? Where did I come from?

So I had to repeat it all over again, how I was looking for her. In response to which I was suddenly assaulted by four or five young females, all yammering at me at once, claiming that they were each as kitten as could be. One almost knocked me back down the skylight trying to drag me away from the others. She hung on one arm and kept saying, "Take me, take me."

You see what a difficult communications problem I was up against here. I had to shake off all those females and repeat that it was a very particular girl I was looking for, not just any old sex kitten, and it was while making this effort that I seemed to have picked up a mere child. A girl of six or seven was clinging to my leg, I found, and no matter how hard I tried to explain it to them, they steadfastly assumed I'd come up here to find any girl, just any girl. "Take her, then," said one old man, "she's a good girl."

What are these people? Savage brutes? To tell a perfect stranger—a member of another race, even— to take from their midst this mere child!

Well, I was no longer afraid. Disgust is all I could feel now. Disgust and astonishment. And I guess this leg of my mission would have been a complete washout if it weren't for one of them who said that maybe *he* knew who I was talking about. Then the crowd parted and let me through, and I found myself talking to that old toothless, light-skinned fellow, the one I'd met on the street below who was almost as white as I am. The others called him "detective," for some strange reason of their own, and he told me he knew a girl who had used the name Kitten, and also Gigi Abercrombie.

"Where can I find her?" I kept asking. "I'm trying to find her."

Then came the crowning touch. Living evidence of how petty and mercenary these people can become. He leered. He bared his ugly gums and leered at me, and he wanted to know how much, how much I was willing to pay for this bit of information.

You can imagine how that made me feel. I'd just been robbed by one of them. He's stolen all the money I had, and now here's this old goat wanting to hold me up again.

Not that I was against paying, but—Thunderation! —when I told them I'd just been robbed, and in this very building, one of them broke into fits of laughter and kept saying, "That's her old man, that's her old man." And that set the rest of them howling, and none of them bothered to let me in on the joke.

Finally the one they called "detective" stopped cackling and got back to the matter at hand. Namely, holding out his upturned palm. So I turned my pants-pockets inside out to prove I had no money and he said it looked like I'd already paid. Which caused a new explosion of laughter. And when that subsided, he said, "Go to the Paradise Hotel and ask for O'Dessa."

But, I told him, O'Dessa is not her name, her name is—

She's wearing a *new* name now, he said.

A *new* name! Well, maybe they change names instead of changing clothes—right?

Be that as it may, there was an emaciated female standing beside him now, and she looked like the very symbol of drug addiction, and she was chattering away about how I'd darned well better bring money with me when I go to find this "O'Dessa" character, because she's a *whore*.

Well, I told them, there's surely some mistake then, because the girl I'm looking for is in show biz.

And when this emaciated girl started giving me a lot of lip about that, the old man turned to her and told her to shut up, and the pair of them got into a loud argument, with the man saying that maybe I

54

could *help* "O'Dessa" because she was in trouble, and the female saying the only thing that would help was money.

And that was about all of this scene I could take. Enough of this . . . charming hospitality, I said to myself, and started making my way back to the skylight. With, I must add, that little girl still clinging to my leg.

And when I got to the skylight, guess what. That character who'd almost done me in by tipping the ladder, he had the unmitigated *gall,* mind you, to ask for a *tip.* He said something like, why didn't I reach my hand inside my *coat* pocket and find him a little tip.

I was sorely tempted to tell him he was darned lucky I *don't* tip. That I don't tip the police to his whereabouts, that the whole bunch of them ought to be thrown in jail for loitering about up here instead of staying inside their own homes where they belong. But I said nothing. Because, well, for some mysterious reason, they were becoming hostile.

So I pried that little girl's fingers loose from my trousers and, with a couple of them yelling that I was a "cold-blooded" so-and-so, I made my way back down that ladder.

Then, while I was feeling my way down that spiral stairway, one of them yelled, "Hey, Sonny! Come back and *kill* him, the"—and good taste prohibits repeating the garble of obscenities she ended that howl with.

Well, I had no idea what that was all about, but I kept my revolver at the ready as I went the rest of the way down, and I certainly was relieved when I made it—out that entrance and into my car. I locked the door and fired up the engine, and I took off like a you-know-what. Back across the river to the *civilized* side of town.

What a relief it was to get across that river. I wasn't about to go to the Paradise Hotel—not tonight. Enough's enough! Tomorrow I'll call the owner. I know Sam Levenstein personally, and as a matter of fact, old Sam owes me a favor or two. I won't beat around the bush with him, either. I'll say, "Sam, there's a girl living in your hotel named O'Dessa. Haul her out and send her to me, quick!"

And then, when I'm face to face with her, that's when the real work will begin. That's when I'll find out a number of things, beginning with, will she or won't she coöperate? If she does coöperate, I'll *save* her from all this—this poverty and squalor they've gotten themselves into here. Yes, I'll save her—provided of course she tells me exactly *who* instigated that insurrection.

Didn't get much sleep Saterdy. They was shootin an yowlin sireens all night long. Towards mornin, a hellycopper come over, liked t'flatten this house with his wind.

Daylight come, I say goodbye t'the little girl I slep with an all them other peoples. Goes downstairs an slip out.

Bumpin up the street mindin my own bizness. Can see peoples up on the avenue so I figure you allowed t'walk t'day.

Oh yeah? Everybody allowed but me! I don't even make it two blocks down the avenue fore this patrol car pulls up. Cop name Cholly—yeah, that's his *name!* Him an some other cop I don't know.

Cholly roll down his winda an he say, Where you goin, Odessa?

Shows my teeth an I lays on my baby-blue voice.

Nowhere, Cholly, jes out walkin. Ain't I allowed t'walk?

Any other a them honky wind-up toys stop me I mighta been okay. But this one steady fuckinover me ever since he got on the force. Tryin t'break me down.

He say, Where's you eye-dee?

Left it back at the hotel.

Say, No eye-dee? In the car, come on.

What for?

Gonna run you in on a dee-oh-pee. No eye-dee.

See what I say? But I knows his game. Leans on his winda, puts a big eye on him an I say, All we gots t'do is go t'my room. My eye-dee's right there.

Here's him, he talking real james bond, he say, Okay. Hop in. Run you over t'the hotel. Check out you room.

She-it. Know what this fool really wants? Wants t'make me his very own pipeline t'the happenings. Man, he ain't got nothin unner that spacehat but pussy an pot—*free* pussy an pot.

Okay, I get in the backseat and we drives down the avenue. Sometimes I dam near feel sorry for Cholly. He got that Mahstahrace sickness. Lookahere, some a them little cholly robot cops can take off them blue rags an be mellow-mellow tricks. But not him. All stretched out, catchin free pussy an pot with one hand, diddlin Big Charlie with the other.

Stops out front a the hotel, leaves the other cop settin in the car an we gets out.

Whoops! Here he is, my ole man. Holdin up the hotel, waitin on me. But he's cool, musta hit his granny for a fix.

Me an Cholly crunch-crunch over the broken glass an go in where the door was. Done shot the glass outa all the doors an windas, every one.

Up the elevator, steady fuckin him in the ear, workin him up.

Last time he ax me t'trick I tole him, Cholly I *caint*. You gots such a powerful bad smell I jes caint. Don't you cops ever wash? Y'all stink so's a girl can smell you a mile away. Comes from bein such punks fo' Big Charlie—so how is I gonna get t'trick with you? Y'all too busy horin for *him!*

He ain't hit on me since. But when he gets t'my room t'day that pistolpackin peebrain got all kinda evil in his head. Say, How come you bed's all made up? Where you sleep last night?

Right here! Got up t'day an made that bed, jes had a feelin you might drop by, bay-ba.

Smiles an he say, Okay take off yer clothes.

I say, Okay lay down twenty dollahs.

You kiddin? I ain't layin down no money, you get out them clothes or I'm takin you in.

Cholly baby, you knows how much I *wanna* trick with you, now *doncha*. But how's I spose t'trick some robot that's steady fuckin with my ass, huh?

James bonds around the room awhile, then he set down on my bed and he say, Odessa I like you. Me an you got possibilities.

Sure enuff? Show me twenty possibilities, twenty green ones.

Stands up an he say, It's jail for you, girl. Let's go.

Thinks I'm gonna do a crumble over that but I jes say, Okay, jail. Grab my purse an I'm on my way.

She-it, I bees safer in jail than out. Give Son a chance t'get his mind on somethin new. Yeah an give this robot t'know he can't pull no jig-jig or jail jive with this hoe. No, an specially with my ole man waitin right outside t'bust my face.

Yeah, that's my choice t'day—the street heat or the

heat-heat. An I'm halfway down the hall on my way t'jail fore I turns an sees Cholly ain't comin. Still back in my room.

Goes back an here's him, he's roamin around sniff-sniff-sniffin. He say, Sniff-sniff what's that sniff-sniff smell? Sniff-sniff you is unner arrest for sniff-sniff narcodicks.

Lord-*dee!* I bout bust a gut laughin. Fall down on that bed an do nothin but laugh.

Think it's funny, eh.

Cholly, I say, you the funniest thing on two legs, walkin around sniff-sniffin like that. Man, you gonna catch a contack an get high's a kite, tryin t'pertend my room's fulla smoke. Ha!

But ole robot still workin. Pulls a roach out his pocket an goes like he jes found it in my ashtray. Ah *ha!* What's *this?* Um-hm, *proof.*

I say, Sweetheart you don't need no proof. Everybody knows you's a stone pothead.

Proof *you* was smokin weed, he say. Eight t'ten years.

Quit tryin t'scare me outa my clothes, you nacheral sack a twenty magic words. You ain't givin me no eight t'ten nothin. You knows dam right well narcodicks season ain't till nex month. An besides, I got me a lawyer now.

Takes off his spacehat an sets on the bed, an he say, Odessa I don't wanna run you in.

Hey, it's gettin pretty risky but I takes one more chance. I hunch it over at him, an I say, Only twenty, bay-ba, an you can kiss my funky pearltongue the rest a the day.

Dam! Looks like he gonna. Lay down twenty an *not* take me in. Runs his hand up my leg an I thunk he was gonna dive in up t'his ears.

But all of a certain he yank his hand out an he say, No! No, I'm *not* layin down *money*.

Pulls his spacehat back down over his ears real slow, still settin on the bed. Say, If that's the way you want it, Odessa.

Tryin t'stall. She-it, I get t-steppin. Gonna take my own self t'jail, he don't hurry an catch up. I'm on the elevator with the door closin fore he gets there.

Goes down t'the lobby an past the man at the desk. I hollers out, Fatdaddy, bolt my room an watch nobody steals my stuff, will ya?

An outside my ole man's still pushin back on the hotel, I sing it out t'the whole street, Find some new thing now, bay-ba, cause this here Mahstah's in Luv with me.

Cholly puts me in the backseat, takes off drivin with the sireen goin. Run me off t'the jailhouse like he's chasin a fire.

Books me on a dee-oh-pee, takes my purse away an hands me over. Same ole ladyguard—she wanna know is I gonna make the phone call, an I tell her yeah, one a these days. She say, You gonna make it now. I say, No. Gonna visit with my friends first. Make that call later, I'll say when.

Locks me in with the other broads an walks off mutterin.

Same ole crowd. Ole home week. An most of 'em got here jes like me, walkin down the street. I tell 'em how Cholly give me that jig-jig or jail jive, they all starts gabbalin over how I oughta get me a good man so's nex cop pulls that can have himself an akseedent.

Naw. I'm sure enuff tired a Cholly upside my ass, but I ain't gonna have him no akseedent. Lookahere, he's straight. Nex cop they send might fixate on boys,

61

an a girl can't work them kind nohow. Like Henry —he's the one cause all this noise.

Tell 'em how I run my ole man out, too, an one a them holes say, Odessa you such a strong-*strong* broad, outlawin like that.

She-it. I ain't that much outlaw. Got me a lawyer, a mellow trick. Gonna call him in three, four days, get back out on the corner makin money like it's goin outa style.

Yeah, but I sure wishes I had me a good man. I don't tell them other bitzes this, but being a lone outlaw in this life, with the johnlaws up one side an the pimps down the other, everybody mouth-waterin for a taste—well you catchin too much mojo at once, it's bound t'cross you up.

Anyhow, we get all the talkin out an then we goes t'playin cards. All day playin cards, all night tryin t'sleep through the dykes. Eatin that rotten jailhouse food and dreamin up hunner dollah tricks by the ton.

Couple days later, jes when I's all set for another day a cards, here come the ladyguard tellin me I been sprung.

Scared the life outa me. Thunk it was my ole man springin me. Tole that guard t'go on back and un-spring me, I ain't leavin this rotten jail—no way! Not for another day or two, uh-uh.

Then Annie-zee—she the one they lets out t'do moppin—she come in right while I'm jawin with the guard, an she say it ain't Sonny, it some whitie out there springin me.

Ooh-wee, must be my lawyer trick, found out I was in, come down here on his own t'get me out. Hot dam.

An I goes out speedin. Guard gotta run t'keep up. Whoops! Take one look at who's waitin an I turns back, smack into that guard's belly. Gonna go right through her if she don't stand aside.

She say, what's the matter now? Don't you know this man?

Yeah, I knows him. Oh yeah, from way back. I say, you ain't turnin me out t'*him*.

Puts everybody in a big hub-bub. This devil, name's Jay See, he say, Come on Kitten, I ain't gonna hurt you. I jes wanna *talk*.

An Cholly—wouldn't you know it, that em-ef's gonna pick now t'be hangin out the station house—he say, *Kitten!* Ah ha ha ha. Hey pussycat, I thought yer name was Odessa.

I shut my mind t'that mothahfuggah. Turn t'Jay See an I say, You gonna bring me back here when you's done? Talkin?

He say, If that's what you want, sure.

Okay, long's you bring me back.

Dam, I sure is strung out. Cholly spacehead tryin t'use me for a dildo on Big Charlie—Sonny tryin t'tear my face t'pieces—an now this Mahstah.

But with simple-ass Cholly robot honkin the wig off me here, I gets the urge t'be gone. Takes the onlyest way. Grab that trick by the arm, turns tail on Cholly —give him t'sniff-sniff a look at what he's missin, steady fuckinover me like he does. An I' struttin out the door like I knows what I'm doin.

Puts me in some veddy veddy Brit-tish kinda sheen, carries me away. Ain't got notion number one where to.

Lord-*dee!* What a dum woolyhead *I* is. Last time I party with this em-ef, I landed in a quarry an dam near drownded.

Drivin along all propped up, stone shutmouth, eyes

63

straight ahead, an pretty soon we's over the bridge an goin down the hiway t'the seashore. Say t'myself, Momma you sure better keep a lookout. This time you ass liable t'land in the ocean.

We's way down this road fore he opens his mouth. Ax me, How you been baby?

Baby! She-it, makes me wanna come back on him makin sounds jes's peckerwood ofay as ole El Beejay.

But I don't. No, better stick with the downhome talk. Don't want him mistakin me for one of his own.

But fore I gets a chance t'answer that baby one, he sayin, You look real good, Kitten.

Curls my tail an I say, So do you-ooh, lover.

Ain't got nothin t'lose. Nothin but my life. So I go on an say, You looks *dee*-licious, bay-ba. But hey, tell me somethin. How come you is springin me? An where you takin me? What a you want me for, huh?

Howja like t'go t'the seashore?

I's goin, like it or not. So I say, How much?

An that brings on his sharptalk. That all you people ever *think* about—money?

I don't know bout all you people, but I sure do know one thing—the game's rigged, fixated. Ain't no other way I can stay alive. Money's air! Money's stone sure enuff air.

Thinks awhile, an he say, Don't worry. You'll make out okay, long's you ko-operates.

Oh, I say, that's my main thing. An I runs it down for him. I say, One hunner's all night, five hunner's all weekend an—

Lookin at me like he got a pain. I quick say, That's a whole lot less'n you can get from them high-ass white broads an I's always open t'nego-sheayshuns.

Relax, he say, you off duty now.

Off duty! You turn off the world an I'm off duty.

64

You fix it so's I can live without money an I's off duty.

Don't you get the pitcher? Kitten I'm ab-ducktin you.

You gonna take *me* in the army?

No, not *in*-ducktin. *Ab*-ducktin.

Now what kinda slant talk he givin me here? She-it, I ain't gonna sit down tight on pride behind *that*. Gonna make this em-ef say it straight out.

So I ax him, Wha's 'at you' doin, bay-ba?

Kidnappin! You unnerstand that? Kidnappin.

Yeah, I unnerstand that okay. An I say, Ma-man, you needs *help*. Kidnappin *me*. Jes who the hell you think gonna buy me back? You is kidnappin the wrong girl. You better turn this car around an take me straight back t'jail an go kidnap you a moneymaker cause you sure ain't gonna make it on *me*.

Takes a deep breath an then he tells it that he ain't kidnappin me *that* way, for money. Oh no, way he kidnappin me is for Luv.

Hey, don't you think I ain't shook behind that. Lookahere, I seen my share a funny-funny tricks in this life. Luv! She-it! This here devil the looniest, the craziest, the twisty-turniest. . . . Oh momma you sure gonna have t'get on some fast dopin out here. Get right t'what he got his meeley little mind on, parlay that to a faree-thee-well.

Yeah, an if he gots in mind some kinda down-the-road, out-in-the-woods whupass kinda luv, he gonna come out that scene with the handle a my steelcomb in his neck. Oh yeah. Hey I'd jump outa this car an walk back if we wasn't gone sixty out in marlboro country.

Get t'work, momma. Quit sittin here gurgalin an get t'work.

Hey lover, I say, *tell* me what yo' got in mind, huh?

65

Come on, run it right on down front so's I can make
. . . you . . . hop-pee. Huh?

Wanna experiment, he say. Wanna get you t'ko-
operate, an if everythin goes well, I wanna *save* you.

Dam, I wish I knowed what he mean by that. Could
be he gamin me somethin awful. But I plays along.
What else can I do? Studies his face for a time, then
I ax him, Is yo' levelin with me?

You bet yer bottom dollah, he say. Looks me straight
in the eye when he says it too.

You mean you wanna look after me an all?

That's right.

An you gonna be good t'me?

That's right.

Sure wishes I had me a bottom dollah t'bet.

Was gonna ax him, does he mean he gonna take me
off the corner. But I didn't. She-it, only one hoe in ten
gets tooked off the corner an I ain't never seen no dude
paddyboy do it. Only musicians, gangsters, cops an
such—mens in the life.

Say t'myself, This man jes cravin black pussy, too
dum t'say it straight out. Yeah, that's all, jes cravin
black pussy. Well that's okay, cause I gots tons an tons
a pussy—all he need is a few pounds a money an we's
in bizness.

Aw, but the whole deal ain't makin no sense. Lookahere, whatever put such noise in his mouth? Ko-operate,
experiment, luv, save me. Do he be havin some day-
dream he's gonna cross over?

Fuggit. What goes out around come back around,
that's a stone sure certain. So whatever this em-ef send
out t'me, gonna lay it right back on him all doubled
up. Yeah, so he better not be some meanass shuckin
an jivin, cause he got himself a woman with nothin
t'lose. Not nothin.

66

I mean t'tell it like it is, I been a-hoein them streets till I's ready. Anythin—see here what I say—*anything* he send out, he gonna get it back double.

Been sittin by thinkin all this out. An the nex time he looks over at me, I say, Okay lover, experiment away.

The whole scheme was sort of an experiment, if you want to know the truth. A multi-level experiment.

Because all I had to go on really was the fact that three years ago she'd alerted yours truly to the existence of another alien and potentially dangerous situation, the so-called I.A.A.P.P. As those who have followed my documentary efforts to date will recall, it was this very woman—known then as Gigi Abercrombie—who put me onto this pre-Hippie type commune, which turned out to be an International Zionist Conspiracy to Communize and Enslave America. She was part and parcel of this front organization that called itself the International Association for the Advancement of Poor People. Or Peaceful People. Or was it Polite People? No matter, the important thing is that it was I—acting on information culled from her—who was instrumental in the enforcement effort that searched out that rats' nest by helicopter, and returned later to relieve our community of its presence.

And just to bring you up to date I might add that she wasn't in that place, their so-called Headquarters, when our peace officers arrived. Not that I feel she should have been taken into custody along with those three Beatnik types, the young men involved. No, because when attractive young women are mixed up in such plots, I much prefer our peace officers weed out the males, the fanatics. Hold them for correction—let the girls seek out new avenues, including the colored.

But I seem to be sidetracking here. I did call Sam Levenstein and he did know of a girl who now calls herself "O'Dessa." And he would have been more than happy to repay me by a quick delivery, if it had not been for one sticky little detail—she was in jail.

This being the case, my next move was clear. I drove to Police Headquarters, which is where our city jail is, and I stomped right into the chief's office. He's another who owes me a favor, and since we've installed the closed-circuit TV system, you can sit in his office and by simply turning the dial have a look at each and every inmate. It's just one of those electronic improvements we've not bothered to publicize—we don't have to *brag* about the way we're advanced.

Well, it was easily verified from the books that there was among their female guests of the moment one registered as "Odessa Smith, Disorderly Person." I made a mental note of the correct spelling of that unlikely name, then I made a few small arrangements with the chief and we tuned in the TV. There she was in this large cell we call the pen, milling around with a lot of other colored women, all gabbing. So I got the chief to release her into my custody, without the usual fine-or-forfeiture deal.

Now perhaps only the really hip reader can appreciate what was involved here. I mean the chances I was taking. Because no matter how much I like this girl as a person—oh and I do like her. As a person, no question about it. I could sit for hours and listen to her talk in that exotic underworld Negro lingo of hers. It's so musical! A perfect delight to the ear. If you can overlook the menace of her certain-certain utterances.

Though I must say there seems something *changed* about her way of talking. She seems to enunciate more clearly now, yet at the same time she seems to be speaking a less standard English than ever before.

But I've changed too, I guess. I'm much more the Hipster now, much less Square—right? It doesn't pay to blow your cool—hip is *in*.

But—getting back to the business at hand—the point I was trying to make is this: She's not exactly the First National Bank when it comes to trustworthiness. Few of them are. I'd hesitate to label her an Habitual Criminal, though it's plain to see she's not a nun. The fact is, I may be letting myself in for trouble here. If she fails to cooperate.

But what would life be without a little gamble now and then? And if she *does* cooperate, the sky's the limit. I mean I just won't hear of letting her go back to jail. That's no reward for virtue, is it? So I've got to be ready with something creative. Something to offer her as an alternative to life as Odessa Smith, Disorderly Person.

And I'd given this problem some thought. Aided, I might add, by the shining example of my good friend and close associate County Commissioner Harry Hooper. A real rugged individualist, old Harry. A higher-up in the John Birch Society and a living demonstration that devout patriotism can walk hand in hand with a little old-fashioned harmless hankypanky.

70

Because besides his *real* wife and family, he keeps this Negro mistress and has fathered children by *her*. I mean just among us white men, you might say Harry's a Classic. And any way you want to cut it, he's a cool daddio. Harry the Hoop, we call him.

But don't get the idea—don't even let it cross your mind that I'm downgrading our own white women. Or detracting from the sacred institution of Marriage. My own marriage isn't exactly a bed of roses—true—but that makes no nevermind. I know perfectly well that one does not escape one's marital obligations by running off with another woman. Especially a woman of another race. And I had no such intention.

On the other hand, my wife doesn't run my whole life. All she asks, really, is that I bring home the paycheck. After that, I can do what I want and she does what she wants. I mean when it comes to equal rights for women, Barbara's a tiger! Refined, intelligent, very highly educated. So of course she has social commitments that won't quit. Women's clubs, charity fundraising—you name it, she's into it. Otherwise she'd just be wasting her wonderful education—right?

So with all this going for her, how can you expect her to keep a tidy home and look after the baby all the time? Or slave over a hot stove all day. Civic duties sometimes keep her tied up till well after dinner time. Therefore, you see, I need a maid. It's not an expense I relish, but what the heck. We're always hiring babysitters and maids anyway, I might as well hire one full-time and let that be that.

Plus the fact that. . . . Well, I don't mean to knock the little woman but we do have a compatibility problem. For one thing, there's a bit of a complication in her past, a rather horrible event involving courtrooms and doctors and investigators. But forget that—the im-

71

portant part is that, being a modern, liberated woman, Barbara flatly refuses to play the role of the submissive female.

Which is all well and good of course. It's just that every once in a while I get . . . carried away, so to speak. And then she gets her back up and accuses me of using her as an end in itself rather than a means, and tells me I should go out and find myself a *sex object,* if that's all I want.

Are you hip? Do you see the possibilities here? I mean it might just work out that I can offer this girl a position as my maid and cook, babysitter, etc. Saving her from a life of disorderliness, while at the same time saving my wife from a life of submissiveness.

Plus information leading to the whereabouts of the enemy within, those certain subversive elements dedicated to overthrowing our way of life.

But I must caution the lay reader not to be impatient. Because in order to get all this set up, I must proceed with a care and a caution. I mean I didn't just drive her to the beach house and bang into a question-and-answer session. We went for a walk first. We had a nice little chat and we got re-acquainted—she met the *new* J. C.

Kidnaps me way down the hiway an off some ole back road, pine trees on one side, ocean on the other. Some crazy house off by itself, sits up on legs, looks over the water.

Parks his car unner the house an he say, Come on, let's take a walk.

What's happenin? He bring me way down here t'ko-operate a walk?

Well that's what we's into now. Leave our shoes in the car and go barefootin in the sand.

Sure is marlboro country. Ain't a soul in sight. Nothin but sand and water. An him.

No tellin what this mothah got in mind, momma, so don't forget t'worry. Hang onto this purse an keep that steelcomb handy.

Pretty soon he gets t'talkin. Say, How you like this place? I owns it Kitten. Own the house an the beach, all up an down as far as the eye can see. Got the papers that say so.

I say, Yeah? Wow bay-ba. An I bigeyes all over him.

She-it, ole Mahstahrace think he own the whole earth. Dum mothahfuggahs, the joke's on them, cause this ole earth owns *them*. Owns everybody. Gonna go on ownin long after him an his papers is six feet in it.

But that's okay. I say, You own the ocean too, bay-ba? All that nice sha-*foom*, sha-*foom* sound them waves makin? Wow, lover, you sure is a rich-*rich* man.

Puffs him out like a toad. Ha! Then all of a certain he's inta *this*, he say, Tell me somethin, what was you doin unner that coat the night a the race riot.

Whoa, hold everythin! That sure do bring me up short. I say, What night? What a you talkin bout?

Night a the race riot. Doncha remember? You was unner an overcoat. Stopped my car, got out an come over an I seen you there. Then somebody jumped out at me an I took off.

That was *you*?

Sure. Didn't you *see* me?

No. Carlights in my eyes.

Oh. Well, he say, what was you doin there in the gutter?

What was *you* doin there in the *car*?

Was my bizness t'be there that night, he say.

You a cop now?

No, heck no. Say, I was there t'obzerve.

Yeah, me too.

She-it, I obzerve jes's much as him, huh.

He say, No foolin, Kitten, when I seen you there that night my heart went out to ya.

Yeah? Wish you'd a stuck it out futher bay-ba. I sure woulda took a hold.

He does a haw-haw over that. An when he all done

laughin, I say, Okay you was nice t'get me out the jail an bring me way down here an *tell* me. Sure do surprise me, how you was the one in that car. Now when you gonna carry me back?

Oh no, he say, we got lots more t'talk about, Kitten.

We do?

Oh, he say, we gotta lotta things t'talk about. Maybe I'm gonna take you out that jail for good.

You doin sivil rights now?

What?

Nothin, forget it. What's all this we gots t'talk about?

Well, he say, I'm gonna tell you somethin that'll really surprise ya. You think I'm white, huh.

Naw, never. Sweetheart yo's as baij as they come.

Quit kiddin. Be serious. Now I'm gonna tell you somethin I never tole anybody else. Last summer. . . .

Yeah?

Last summer I went t'see my sister.

Oh, you gots a sister. Fine.

Yes an she jes had a baby last summer. That's why I went t'see her—my wife was pregnant.

You went t'see you sister's baby. Big deal!

Yes, an I couldn't *believe* it.

Believe what—the *baby?*

Yes, because . . . because—because he's part Nee Grow!

Huh?

He's not *white.* He's a *non*-white. My own nephew, part Nee Grow.

What happen? You sister marry a spade?

He spits it out—*Course* she didn't marry a *spade!*

Not even for one night?

She marry a sweed. Pure sweed.

Um-um. Well you know that ole sayin—mamma's baby, poppa's maybe.

75

No! No queshun about it. That sweed gotta be the father.

Okay that sweed's the father. Now who's the sire? Some people has a dozen daddies while they's growin up an not one a them daddies is the sire.

But he shakin his head no no no. Say, That sweed's the sire, baby looks jes like him. Chip off the ole block, except . . . he's part . . . he's part . . . Nee Grow.

Oh them sweed's is swingin mixers.

No, not this one. My brother-in-law's pure sweed, family tree goes *way* back. Abso*loot*ly no African blood.

Well then you sister's—

An I shut my mouth. Ain't gonna be the one t'say it. Not t'*him*. Way out here in nowhere.

Hey, lots a spades runnin with the ofay, makin out they's jes's bright white an dead right as ole El Beejay. That ain't news t'*me*. You watch the tee vee sometime when George Wallass come on, take a good look at him an dig the black bones unnerneath his husslin white front. All that passin ain't news t'me but I ain't gonna be the one t'break it t'*him*.

Specially the way he lookin down on me with his face all scrinched up. Dam near cause me t'laugh. But I say, Wha's a matter bay-ba?

Do you *ree*lize? Kitten, don't you see? That makes *me* part Nee Grow.

Sure is the wrong part. Says it like he gonna cry over it. Anyhow, what's he want outa me behind that—a soul brother sweatshirt?

Hell I don't know what t'say. Usually I gots a come-back, but I'm sure enuff stuck this time.

Onlyest thing I gots in mind is t'quit this prominod-din for seagulls an get goin in the other direckshun. So I struts around in a circle for a few turns, makin out

I'm thinkin it all over. An when I gots him t'followin I heads back towards the car an the house.

Then I commence runnin my mouth. I say, Man that sure musta put you through some funny-funny changes, huh. But she-it, don't sweat it. You's part Nee Grow but you's all white all right. Me, I's part Nee Grow too, but I's the black-step-back part. Other side a the line. Happens all the time. Don't have a thing t'do with nothin. All it gets down to is, the grandmommas and the grandpappas got some color in they lovelife, but it didn't do a thing t'take away the line.

Ain't hardly hearin what I'm sayin. Got his head down an his feet kickin sand, painful look on his face. Painful.

I say, Hey man, don't let it worry *you*. Nobody ever put you down for a black man. Lots a brothers an sisters got kinfolk lighter'n you is.

But he say, Shock a my life! Couldn't eat, couldn't sleep. Was afraid my own son was gonna come out lookin Nee Grow. Thought I'd lose my *mind*.

Ain't that a bitch? How can he lose what he ain't never found?

I say, Well what color's you son? He come out Nee Grow?

Oh no, he say. Looks jes *fine*. Blond, blue eyes.

She-eee-eee-*it!* The part this em-ef is Nee Grow is some part black peoples sure don't need.

But I cool it an I say, Wha's yo' boy's name? Tom? Is he gonna grow up t'be a big bad see-eye-aye man an keep the world safe fo' Missy Ann's fur coat?

He say, What the heck you talkin bout? I can't unnerstand you when you talk like that.

Nothin, forget it.

Well quit talkin dialeck an speak so's I can unnerstand!

77

Ain't no way he can unnerstand. No way in life. But what the hell is I sweatin his crazy slant talk for? Part Nee Grow. She-it! Momma better get t'work an see can she snap this sad-ass part-man jazz an make some cents.

So I say, Hey you ever hear the one bout the spade goes shoppin for a washin machine? He say t'the salesman, How come all these here washin machines is white? Y'all prejudice? An the salesman say, No we ain't prejudice. Take a look inside these washin machines. Each an every one got a black agitator inside.

Does that make him laugh? Hell no. Jes looks disgusted.

Some experiment. Gonna be all day draggin over his part Nee Grow jive. What kinda down-at-the-mouth shuckin an high-ass foolery goin on here, anyhow? Sure hope he don't start callin me sister, cause I ain't no where near callin him brother.

Be havin me a good laugh, he wasn't lookin so sad. Part Nee Grow. But what can I do behind him breakin down over that? Hmmm, let's see can I cool down his mind.

I say, Hey baby, you know how the tee vee's always talkin race? They got the space race, political race, boat race, auto race, black race, white race . . . but you wanna know somethin? The onlyest real race in the whole world is the who's gonna make it t'mellow yellow first race, the brights in the sun or the spades in the shade? Yeah, that's the big-big race.

Kitten, he say, I *tole* you I can't unner*stand* you when you talk dialeck!

Ga-*dam*! This em-ef ain't ready for *nothin*! Okay then, if I can't do nothin else with his mind, let's see can I fuck with it.

I say, Hey you wanna know somethin else? When **a**

78

man screws a sheep, I say—an I'm speakin so up-tight white he oughta get it through his skin if his ears can't pick it up—I say, when a man screws a sheep, do you know what happens? That sheep has a half-human chile. Yeah. Is yo' hip t'sheep peoples, bay-ba?

Here's him, he lookin popeyed. Say, No no no, that's entirely impossible! Besides, sex with sheep is outlawed.

Yeah? How come? Don't the govermint want sheep peoples? How bout dogs? You allowed t'do it with a dog?

An he snarls like one. Don't be re-*dick*yalus.

Lord-*dee!* He ain't nowhere *near* ready. All I'm tryin t'do is lighten this part man's Nee Grow burden an lookahere, I gots him snarlin at me.

Fuggit, I give it up an I throws back my head an I lets go a big laugh.

Lookin down on me real quizzical now. Say, How come you color people got so much t'laugh about?

Gee-ee-*zuz!* Dam near put me inta the fallin down laughin *fits*. At his scrunch-up of a face. On top a how flatout broke I is.

Momma, this scene ain't making you no richer. Better change it, get back t'my main thing.

So I say, Come on. An I'm sputterin so bad I can't hardly get it out. I say, Let's go up t'your house an take off our clothes. I ain't never seen no man like you, all white an part black. I gots t'find out is you a checkerboard or does you got stripes?

It's a funny thing, but sometimes I feel like a man behind bars. Sometimes I get an urge to just quit the ratrace, give it up, be a bum the rest of my life.

I make a good living, sure. For a guy my age, I make an excellent income. But am I happy? I sometimes wonder. Our home, stocks, bonds, her Ford, my Jag . . . if it wasn't for the excitement of my own real estate ventures, it would all come out to one great big dull *blah*. Sometimes, when I get depressed I think Heck, if this is all there is ever going to be to my life, I might as well forget it. Take a hunk of change and move to some undiscovered island in the tropics.

But there *aren't* any undiscovered islands any more, and I can't really *afford* to give up my position. I've worked too hard to secure it. And now that we've got a good solid two-party system with both parties in full agreement about all important issues, I'd be a *fool* to walk away from it. I'm deeply involved in providing the community with effective political leadership. Including police protection.

Yet I don't really feel . . . how should I say it? Well, I just feel there's something missing. But how can that *be?* I'm twenty-four years old and up to my ears in real estate. If only one of my land deals pays off I'll be set for life.

Like I told Kitten as we strolled the beach, I own all she can see—the beach house and the waterfront for a stretch of seven miles. Naturally this awed and overwhelmed her. But it's nothing, really. With my inside track at the Courthouse, I may end up a millionaire. It's all in knowing who is going to want which pieces of land for how much and when.

Take this piece of beachfront: The previous owner didn't have the brains to realize its possibilities, so he failed to pay the taxes and I got it for a song. Now all I have to do is twiddle my thumbs and keep the price up, and if nobody else can afford it, I'll sell to the federal government.

Of course I hate the federal government as much as the next guy and I know it shouldn't have all that power. But you've got to be realistic. The federal government isn't going to quit bilking the taxpayers, so why fight it? Get a piece of the action, baby, because if you don't, somebody else will. That's how I see it.

Not that I was confiding all this to her, but it was on my mind. God's own beautiful beach, and it's all mine. And the only house on the whole seven-mile stretch is mine. Until I get an offer I can't resist. My contractor just put the finishing touches on it last week. Installed the phone Friday.

Don't know why Barbara can't stand it here. I fear, though, that last weekend was her first and last visit. She couldn't wait to get back to the city Saturday night. Of course she went on at a great rate, giving me this tongue-lashing about how I'd left her there all alone when I went to the riot. But she never liked the idea of the beach house from the start. Said it's too primitive. And Sunday afternoon, she accused me of going to the Negro ghetto *not* for the riot, but because, she said, I only want some quote Black Nigger Bitch unquote. Then she rhymed bitch with beach and told me I could take said bitch to the "bitch" house and "go native" for all she cares.

Funny how life works out. Here I am strolling along with a dark-skinned girl, barefoot, feeling very much like I have indeed gone native. Yes, and feeling damned good about it, too. Even found myself confiding in her. Couldn't resist telling her it was *me*, the night of the riot—I was the one who found her hiding under that old overcoat. Well, you should have seen her expression when I broke that news. Absolutely flabbergasted!

No need to go into what else we talked about. Nor what she had to say. *The New York Times* she ain't. But we did enjoy each other's company, despite our many basic differences. Different living patterns, different moralities, different. . . . Well, there are differences that won't quit. That's what makes America great.

Which reminds me. Another thing I wanted to discuss with her was the role of the Negro. But I put it off. I mean, it's perplexing how the Negro just has not taken advantage of his opportunities in this country. The Irish have, and so have the Italians, the Jews, the Poles, and all the rest of them. So why does the Negro hang back? Demonstrating in the streets, obstructing traffic, moaning "We Shall Overcome," and finally causing violence in their own neighborhoods.

You can't say we don't hire them—when they're

qualified. Take myself, for example. I'm prepared to hire her at a moment's notice. As soon as I'm sure she'll cooperate.

Which I tried to determine when we returned from our stroll on the beach and went inside. I was trying to figure out a way to talk with her about the riot. I mean I wanted a very frank and open discussion of it. Especially its cause. But I couldn't just bluntly bring up the subject. You know how they'll bend over backwards to fool white people. So I tried to sneak up on it by discussing the dangers of an enemy takeover.

Well, I'm afraid she didn't quite comprehend what I was talking about. She seemed a bit confused about the enemy within. And what she had on her mind was a communication of a more basic nature, and she's not at all inhibited, you know.

So I finally decided that the only way to score was to deal with her at her own level. To approach my subject from the bottom up, you might say. I would have preferred to discuss the enemy within first, but she's definitely a very wild chick. And she left me with no other choice, really. I was forced to let her have her way.

She certainly can be . . . how should I say it? Downright unpatriotic and disrespectful of our sacred national colors, that's what. Some of the remarks she made about our flag and national commitments were almost beyond belief! Under different circumstances, I'd have come down on her with both feet. But, I decided, one step at a time—later I'll teach her the meaning of American freedom.

Hey, what a place. Everythin brand-spankin, hope-t'die new. Fireplace with wood all stocked up nice. Big big sofa an sink-down chairs. Bedroom an a kitchen that's outa sight. Dishwasher, built-ins. Push-pull, click-click.

Might's well make myself t'home. I know tricks with some mellow pads, but I ain't never got me one good as *this*. Man, this place makes me plain *hoo*ngry! Everythin's so neat I could jes start in grazin on the funicher.

Checkerboard man, I say, you got a woman t'go with this house?

Wa-el, he say, I *am* married.

That's okay. I sends my tricks home bettern they comes t'me.

Good, he say, cause I have a very—wonderful—*wife*.

Why's he say it like that? Tryin t'lowrate me? Tryin t'play one broad off a'gin the other? She-it, he better not. Ain't a square broad goin with a game sharp's mine. Well I can feed a man better, sweet talk him sweeter, clean a house neater, an it's a stone sure certain I can groove with him better in bed. The day I can't outsharp some wife, that's the day I give up horin.

Fuggit, forget it. This place gone right t'my nacher. Gots t'let my pussy know she's out the jailhouse now. Feel like sayin, Man I got such a hot one t'lay on you, gonna lowrate your ole lady without even gamin her.

Can't wait t'work out. Shuck my clothes an hop in that baffroom, take a fullout shower, wash the jail off my skin an the funk outa my moneymaker.

Squeeky clean, all set t'ko-operate to a fare-thee-well.

But uh oh. He ain't made a move. Still settin on the sofa, dressed fo' church. Well here I come struttin, all spiffed up in my blackass birthday suit.

Say, Wait a minute, Kitten. First I wanna ask you somethin. We got a problem in this country, y'know. The enemy within. Now you don't want the enemy t'take over here, do you?

Mothahfuggah, I tell him, way I's feelin right now, that enemy can't get in fast enough.

What? You *do* want the enemy t'take over?

Oh geezuz. I floomp down in a chair an I say, Fuggit. The ofay done tooked over.

What? *Who* took over?

I smiles, an I say, Hey comere an take *me* over.

Oh Kitten, be serious.

I *is* serious!

The Commonists, the Commonists—we got t'guard against the Commonists! Aren't you afraid?

Ooh-wee! He could drag that out fo' daze. So I up an

move my blackass over on the sofa side a him, an I say, Lookahere what's taken you over. You afraid?

But he still got his tongue flip-floppin on the Commonists like some kinda hooked fish. Look at the vee-et cong! *That's* why we got a military innervenshun in the far east.

Gonna rank this shit somehow. I stands up in front a him an I say, Hey baby, dig this here *cum*minest. Forget the far east, get you a military innervenshun right here. Come on, get that pretty flip-floppin where it'll do some good in this world.

But still he don't make a move. Well if I gots t'rape him, that's what I'll do. Lay the blame on mother nacher.

But who's he think he foolin? I see that lump. So I jes finely grab that zipper an fish him on out. Say, Okay baby, you wanna preach? Well do it with this—that's the onlyest kinda sermon I'm gonna hear. You wanna preach the enemy within? Then get him in. Come on, rise up and get you a military innervenshun right here. Leave them far east Commonists alone, put him after *my* cumminest, lover.

Then I jes grab a-hold an haul him off the sofa, *drag* him inta the bedroom. Got me feelin so *eee*vil I'm ready t'rip the clothes off him. An if he don't give it to me quick, I'm gonna sure enuff hop on an take it.

Dam near have t'pull him on t'get him mountin innerpussy innervenshun. Lay that jail-starved cumminest on, an I tells that man, Get at it, mothahfuggah. Get that innervenshun goin, cause you's inta the biggest, baddest, *thee* most squirminest, oh *thee* most eeevil cumminest for miles an miles. Ding dong the everlovin cong, ole puss is slurpin up that innervenshun like a hungry hog. Oh root 'em out, Mahstah Military, inner-fo'-criss-sake-*veen*. Preach t'me, lover, tell me how's he doin, this enemy within. He's ofay but that's okay—don't you never tell no brothers but right now I'm a stone freak for blue eyes.

Puttin out cumminisms like they gonna take over the whole bedroom. Ooh-*wee!* Niagra Falls! With a dead log floatin around in it.

Here's him—all reared up lookin down on me like he never seen a woman go for herself. Don't know why he's holdin back, but that's okay—way I'm feelin, he can jes keep that enemy within. I'll rest up awhile an work out again.

Yeah, but the next thing he do, he rolls off. Well I don't feel so good about that. Ain't gonna rank no square broad this way.

Layin side a me, flagpole steady stickin straight up, starin at the roof.

I say, Hey there military, ole innervenshun sure did ding dong the everlovin cong. Any time you wanna get you another cumminest, you jes get t'preachin. Sock it to 'er, cause I gots cumminists that won't quit.

An here's him, he scrunch up his face an he say, Why do you have t'talk unpatriodick?

Who's unpatriodick! Lookahere the nice flagpole you got. Red white an blue. Red head, white skin, blue veins. An the onlyest thing ole flagpole gots is a shine. Mine. After the Commonists so hard he ain't made it t'the cumminests. Hey baby, whataya say we dance that flagpole down. You wait right here, I'll fetch a cocktowel an be right back.

Direckly I'm washin him up with nice warm water, wipin him off, soft an easy.

Bout time I use my head. See can I get ole flagpole flappin in the breeze. Hummin the star spangle banner—hummin an hummin till he jes got t'salute. Jes enough t'get his mind off the Commonists an put him after my cumminest again.

Then I say, Hey Mahstah Military, let's get another war goin, huh? Come on, you ain't got the last a my cumminest.

That gets a little smile outa him, an pretty soon we got a new innervenshun. Preachin like he means it now. Groovin. Reachin t'fetch some more a what I done save up in the jailhouse.

Workin out so good it jes turns on my hollerin. Yeah I'm ballin. Yellin. Ooh-ooh Check-er-board. Gun fo' that cumminest, mothahfuggah. Rat-a-tat-tat you es-oh-be, sock it to 'er! Ding dong the *nasty* ole cong, he's in this jungle, you *know* he is. Sweet geezuz, get t'steppin—don't let 'em get away—dance his ass, baby —fetch 'em out an *stomp* 'em. Ooh-ooh-ooh, here he *comes!*

An there goes my second. *Whew!*

Him? Looks like he thinks I done tooked his military right out the game. She-eee-eee-it. Momma, what's the matter here? Why can't you grab this bulldog's tail an get him barkin? Get you hoein blackass in gear or he gonna fuck you in the ear! With Commonists!

Well I been trickin long enough t'know when t'quit goin for myself an read signs. Figure the way he bees handlin me, I better troll the bottom, put some keyster in his way, see can I stir up what he's freaky for. So I turn some slow low phillydog bitchin on him, jes teasin, testin him out.

Whata you tryin t'make me *do?*—that's him.

Lord-*dee!* I swear t'god an allah both, this man's so all blocked up an fulla plugs, I gotta turn loose my whole self an dam near climb over an under, an he got all the cumminests I'm ready t'give for awhile. Onlyest thing I ain't put on him is the magic words.

So that's what I do—turn on a recordplayer worth a magic words. Same time I reach back an grab that military an get him innerveenin from behind.

Ha! You oughta seen that man come alive behind that game. Them magic words is knockin down blocks an pullin out plugs till he's belly-spankin my ass to a fare-thee-well. Me, I jes keep on hootin like I'm gonna cuss the whole house down.

Finely! At last!

Thunk for awhile this military was clear outa ammunishun. He sure do need some re-activatin. Plain an fancy. Healthy man with a head fulla Commonism—somethin musta done took the spirit from him.

Most likely a woman. Some a them squares'll bed down with a man one night an have his jock tied around his neck by mornin. Make him look like the one on the telephone book. Won't untie him till he brings home his paycheck, then tie him up again the next night. Maybe this here ole trick a mine done married hisself to a woman like that.

Hmmm. I'm gonna make him a steady an get him mellow back, I sure got some re-activatin t'do. Well no time like the now, so I say, Hey Checkerboard, when you wind up an go fo' you'self, you sure do give momma some milk fo' the baby.

Smiles a little.

I say, Sweeten me up real nice, yes sir. Anytime you wants this woman t'come in this house an treat you good, you jes—

Yeah, he say, *yeah!* That's exackly what I want—want you t'stay here, be my made.

Whoa! Hold it, back up some. I ain't no made, I's a hoe. Baby, I don't make beds, I muss 'em.

Ah, Kitten, he says, I'm gonna *save* you from all that.

Sure enuff? Wanna keep me all night? That bees another fifty on top the one I got comin now.

Looks at me like he don't know what I'm talkin about. She-it, always did have trouble with this one. I'd be rollin all over his pants if I had a way outa here.

But the way it is, I cool it. Ain't got nowhere t'go if I could get out, no way t'get there. Only back t'jail, cause I owes a week's rent on my room. The Man ain't gonna let me in broke. Might's well glide along here, see can I parlay what I got, get what I ain't got later.

One thing sure—he oughta have some food in this place. So I say, Mmmm, Checkerboard, I's *hoo*ngry.

Has hisself a laugh. Say, *Hoo*ngry! Never heard anybody say it like *that* before.

Yeah well I's jes a dum nigger bitch, don't know no better. Caint talk no way sep woollyhead downpeoples talk. Come on, let's get up an fix us somethin t'eat. Been on jail slop till my belly's mostly rust. Feels like I'm all holes an empty spaces.

Leave him layin in bed gigglin, go trippin off t'the kitchen like I been droppin Tru. Stone mellow behind takin my pussy out the jail.

But huntin in his cupboards brings me down some. Nary a thing here but facktry food. Deehydrated this an frozen that. Food t'make money on, nothin t'eat.

Makes me so mad I walk t'the bedroom door an I say, Come on, Checkerboard, get dressed. We gonna find a store, buy somethin t'eat.

Naw, he say. Plenty a food here. Look in the kitchen.

I look-did in the kitchen—ain't nothin there. Come on, let's step out. You ever had any real good down-home food? You's part Nee Grow—you needs some food from the ole country so's you can tell one part

90

from the other. Take me shoppin an I'll put some food in your belly'll give you so much soul you'll take on a year-round suntan.

Dam near gots t'package him, fore he's in his clothes again. Back out his veddy veddy British, take off t'find a market.

Well then, let's skip the gory details of our tryst, shall we? And now it's approaching dinnertime. Kitten (or should I call her Odessa?)—anyway, she marches in her altogether out to the kitchen and rummages around in the cupboards, and in spite of ample evidence to the contrary, she declares that there's no food here.

Which is perfectly ridiculous. I stocked up Friday. Filled those shelves to overflowing. There's canned goods, frozen goods, soaps, detergents, pots, pans, dishes, the works! Enough for a month.

But we must go shopping—she *insists!* And rather than hinder the progress I'm making so far (toward winning her confidence so she'll tell me who instigated that race riot), I let her have her way.

Although this does present a bit of a problem. Owing to our color difference, you know. I mean, should I go shopping, or should I lend her the Jag so she can go?

Because the only third alternative is that we both go together. And in this bailiwick, that might prove spectacular.

On the other hand, why shouldn't I do it that way—take her shopping? I mean if I can find some place at that shopping center to buy her a maid's uniform. Get her in a maid's uniform, I reasoned, and we can both go into that supermarket together and still be cool. Some of our best people take their maids shopping.

So we drove to the shopping center, which is a few miles down the road and inland a bit, and on the way I brought up the subject of the maid's uniform. And guess what. She took it as an insult! Said she isn't a maid, she's a prostitute. Said she doesn't make beds, she musses them.

J. C., I said to myself, you have a little challenge on your hands here. This filly needs breaking in before she'll be domestic. Her deep disregard for our flag and foreign commitments, and now *this*. That's all right, though. It's a little challenge now and then that keeps life stimulating—right? Like I always say, where would the FBI be without the Communist Party? Every pro needs a con.

But, I discovered, there was nowhere at that shopping center to buy a maid's uniform. So, as fate would have it, I ended up handing her ten dollars and sending her into the supermarket alone.

Gadzooks, I thought as I waited in the parking lot. What kind of a fool am I? Giving a Negro girl ten dollars—no telling what she might do with that money.

But after a while the supermarket's electronic doors popped open and here she came pushing a shopping cart, and it looked like she must have shoplifted two dollars for every one dollar's worth she bought. I mean, she went in with ten dollars and came out with three big shopping bags full! Well, she must have spent some of her own money too, I guess.

And what a mess of produce she got. Lettuce, peppers, carrots, onions, all kinds of vegetables and fruits. Plus an assortment of exotic spices and hot sauces and whatnot.

I was chuckling to myself about this as I drove out of that shopping center—how she was making life difficult for herself, buying the kind of stuff you have to lean over a hot stove about. When I happened to glance in the rearview mirror and notice a police car behind us. At first I thought nothing of it, but when I made the turn onto the Old Bay Road and this patrol car made the same turn, I began to wonder.

At which point, Kitten said he was following us because of the difference in our color, and my palms began to sweat.

The next thing you know, his blinker was on and he was signaling me over to the side of the road. I got out of the car to greet him, you know, with a friendly smile and all. I mean, it was all very absurd. I hadn't broken any traffic regulation and what business is it of his if I want to take my maid shopping?

Well, the trouble is, he knew *of* me but he didn't know me personally. And he became a little surly. Said, "Routine check. Let's see your car registration."

I got that out for him, plus my driver's license, and I figured that would put an end to it. But no! It seems he didn't trust what he saw. Put through a call on his radio-phone for them to run a *make* on me.

"What are you planning to do?" I joked. "Run me in?"

And was amazed to hear him reply: "That's right. Going to hold you on suspicion."

"Suspicion of *what?*"

"Suspicion of auto theft and impersonating an official of Hook County," he had the gall to say.

I was stunned. Speechless.

"Unless," he added, "you can prove who you are."

Prove who I am! Well, I hauled out my billfold and took out every ID I own. Credit cards, club cards, all of it. And he wasn't satisfied that I am who I am until he saw my picture on one card. He peered closely at this photo and then at me, back and forth awhile. And finally—finally, he let me go.

Oh, he apologized—sure. Said it was the girl I was with that threw him off.

"She's my maid," I kept saying. "I just hired her. Haven't had time to get her a uniform yet. Just showing her where the shopping center is."

All right then, I took his name and number and we continued on our way back to the beach house. I must admit I was a bit shaken by the incident. Imagine, *me* stopped by a peace officer! Without due cause, right here on a road that runs along my own property! What did he think he was doing—protecting my property from me? Or me from my property? I mean, sure he made a mistake—*but*. I've never been on the wrong side of the law in my life. Any observant officer should be able to see that by just looking at me. And who I'm with does not give a peace officer due cause. I'm still me.

Well, it certainly was a lesson. I vowed to get this girl a maid's uniform at the very first opportunity. And I'll not take any more guff about her being a prostitute not a maid. She'll wear a uniform or else.

Otherwise, my mission to save her won't work. After all, we can't go around being stopped by peace officers all the time, can we?

We finds that supermarket okay. But he give me a ten an tell me he ain't goin in with me. Too much specktackle, he say.

She-it. Too scared t'fuck with Sam's setup.

I tell him, Man nobody gonna take you for part Nee Grow. You the whitiest whitie goin. Somebody in there don't like us bein diffrent shades, that's *his* hangup.

But he won't go.

Okay, I tell him he ain't gonna be along t'say what he likes. An I goes in myself t'do it.

That ten don't take me very far. Pick up some greens an stuff t'make flavor an that's all the futher it'll go. Won't take me t'the meat counter.

Carry it back out, load it in the truck an we drives away.

Then, out on the road, some cop hits on us. Pull us over an made Jay t'show his eye-dee.

I don't say nothin but I tricked this cop. He sneaks

over an buys black pussy at the Paradize now an then, an he party with me one time. One a them Mahstah-race mohnstahs. I gamed him for his wristwatch. Sonny wearin it now.

Time that cop quits fuckinover Jay an lets us drive on, ole Checkerboard got a mouthfulla nastiness. Ga-zoopin this an ga-zoopin that all the way home. Steady sayin he gonna put me in a made's uniform.

Carries the bags up the steps an I goes in the kitchen an starts makin supper.

But him, he's badmouthin all over the house. Finely I can't take it no more, I holler out, Watch yo' language, mothafuggah!

Ha! That slow him down.

I say, Don't you know you ain't spose t'growl an snarl thisaway? In front of a lady? An lookahere, you can jes forget that made's uniform right now. Onlyest thing gonna keep the fuzz off me is put me in a white skin. So come on, take all that stuff off you mind, take 'em off like they was clothes an hang 'em in a closet. Put you mind on what momma's brewin up. Yeah, cause I don't do this for every paddyboy dude trick. Get in here an show me some 'preciation. This here food ain't rolled out no facktry for moneymakin, it growed up in the earth for folks t'eat.

Well that turns him around. Comes up behind me an puts his arms around, give a snuggle. An he say, I'm beginnin t'like this, Kitten. Better an better.

Huh. I don't say nothin but I sure do notice. This man got a powerful need for a good lovin woman. Yeah but thinkin back on it he always did have.

Now he's hangin round gladeyein me. Glintin an flashin. Remind me a them mens hangs out at the Para-dize—we calls 'em hozes—an I'd sure be headin for trouble if he was. This house an him an gettin back

97

t'some good downhome soul food after all that crap in jail—man, I's a *soff* one t'night. All I needs is a smoke an I bees mellow.

Hey, come t'think of it, I maybe got some smokes. In the linin a my purse. Police done give me back my purse t'day an if they'd a found my stash a weed they'd a sure enuff stoled it, purse an all.

Got supper goin good now so I say, Hey wait right here, ma-man, don't go way.

Chop-chop in the livinroom, check out my purse. Here it is. Papers an all. Stuck up in the linin.

I hollers in, Hey Jay let's get high.

You know what? He thinks I mean booze. Ha! He say, Yeah! Goes rattlin round in this here bar he got tween the kitchen an the livinroom, pulls out a bottle an starts pourin.

Oh well, to each his own. Pours out two glassfuls a skoch, drops icecubes, hands me one.

I say, Thank eeyoo deah. Ex-scuse me pleeze.

Hops in the baffroom an rolls myself a helper. Bout t'fire up in the baffroom, but then I say t'myself, she-it. Might's well smoke it right down in front a him. Yeah. What's he gonna do about it?

Carries it out an puts myself in the chair cross the room from his an here's us, he's drinkin an I'm smokin.

Looks over an he say, What kinda cigaret is that?

This is a roll-yer-own kind.

Got a peeculear smell.

Yeah, it's the makin's.

Oh? What kinda makin's?

Ummm, Turkish.

Oh. Well, he say, I don't smoke. Gave it up.

That's good, cause them cigarets cause cancer. That's the story that's out now. Me, I only smokes this here roll-yer-own kind.

You certainly do inhale deep.

Uh-huh.

Then he smile an say, Drink up. Let's have another. When's dinner gonna be ready?

Time supper's on, we both mellow. An he like that supper fine, too.

Tried t'get him t'put more sauce on his, but he say, Too hot!

Well I let it go—to each his own.

After we's done eatin, he shows me how t'run the dishwasher. Was gonna go ahead an stick the dishes in himself but I ain't never runned a dishwasher an I say, Hey let me do that. You get a woman in here, you oughta stand back and let her do her thing, quit tryin t'put her aside.

Get the dishwasher goin an we's settin in the livinroom again, he say, Hey Kitten, remember when I seen you last, you was livin at some place call the eye double aye double pee—what ever happen t'that place? You ain't livin there no more?

Oh, I say, the fuzz fell on that place. I was singin at the Fish Pond when they done it.

That's all I tell him. Don't like t'talk about it. Cops sure did pull a real bigtime bust. Surround that place an *had* themselves. Tole everybody come out, come out with they hands up. Beat everybody up, throwed 'em in jail.

All I knowed that night was nobody come t'pick me up an carry me back out there. Slep in the city that night an the nex day I trick some detective an he tole me.

Johnlaw give 'em a floatout an only three came back t'town. Herk, Mary Lou an Hap.

Now Mary Lou's on the needle an Herk's put away on a phoney sex charge, an Hap got put away for tryin t'live with the brothers an sisters. Johnlaw took him for a crazy. Tole 'em he'd rather live on our side then the white side. Kep stoppin him an harrassin him till he blowed his top an mouthed off, then they took an put him away for bein in sane.

But I don't tell ole Checkerboard all this. I ax him, I say, You never tole nobody bout that headquarters, did you?

Naw! He say, What bizness is it of mine?

I don't know but we always was wonderin who blowed the whistle, cause we sure wasn't doin no harm out there—like books. Hey Jay, lookahere all the books you got. You know what we use t'do at the eye double aye double pee? My man use t'read from these books out loud.

Laughs an he say, I jes bet! I'll bet you had a real *raw* colleckshun, huh. Tell me, what'd he read, this friend a yours? Dyry of a French Stenograffer?

Puttin me on. Thinks all Hap read was sex books. So I fuckup his mind a little. I say, Oh he read workers a the world unite, nothin t'lose but you chains, shit like that.

Looks like he seen a ghost. Ha! I knowed he be scared a them words. But I jes ack dum's a headscarf, billyclub upside it.

He tryin t'ack cool, he say, Very innerestin. What else he read?

Can't rezist fuckin with him jes one more time. I say, Oh he read some books say everybody oughta own a fair share a all the moneymakin stuff so's everybody's cut in for a little taste an nobody gets left out.

Ah ha! Very very innerestin.

An he look like he seen two ghosts.

She-it, I could have a nacheral ball messin this mothahfuggah's mind, sayin things he ain't allowed

100

t'think. But I let it go. Don't know why it scares him so. Do he think them words gonna take away his gig? Anyhow, I don't wanna scare him too much. So I say, Oh yeah, that readin was nice. Use t'make me real mellow, like music.

What else you read out there, he say.

Oh, read Shakespeer an Throw an Markey Desod. Come on, pull down one a them books an do some readin now, huh?

Then all of a certain he brighten up an he say, Tell ya what, Kitten. I gots some books in the bedroom. Come on.

Goes in there an he pulls open a drawer, takes out a pile a pitcher books show peoples workin out all kinda diffrent ways, every page a new freak party.

I say, Ooh-wee, baby, let me *see!*

An we bellies down on the bed an goes through 'em. He steady askin, you ever do it like this, an you ever do it like that? An pretty soon we's hotter'n a pair a roasted chestnuts.

An this time when we sets that military innervenshun goin after the cumminests, we is right t'gether.

Got this man re-activatin pretty good. Hey, an I's a long way outa jail myself. Keep this up an we's gonna be the baddest cumminests for miles an miles.

Hop in the shower t'gether an wash each others down real nice an we gets all soaped up an do the bellyrub, an then we jes stand an let the water rain down awhile.

Hop out an dry each others off with big soff towels, an we end up feelin so groovy we jes crumble-tumble inta bed, an fore I even got time t'think about it we's sleepin doublespoon with the ocean sha-foom, sha-foom. An I ain't got my hunner for the night!

Clean forgot that hunner, cut right into a dream.

Yeah I'm havin this crazy dream that I'm shoppin like a suburb housewife. Off the corner an all squared up, wheelin round some big ole shoppin center, buyin stuff for this here house, carryin it in, cookin, goin through all this suburb housewife jazz, happy as a pumpkin.

This dream carry me right through t'mornin. Woked up an here's him, he's up an speedin around. Say, Gotta hurry, gonna be late for work.

Musta been that dream was still strong in me. I got up an went t'playin Dagwood an Blondie. Put on the coffee, got him a couple a quick eggs. Stood over him whilst he gobbles it down an I follows him out the door t'wave goodbye.

An here's me—he's vroomin away in his car an I'm standin on the top step naked as a jaybird wavin at him—an *then* I remember.

Gee-zuz, you dum bitz! Who you think you is? You let the man get off without payin! An now you ain't even got no way out this marlboro country!

She-it, jes cause the man need a woman here, that don't make your own bee-you-tee-ful blackass *it*. Wake up, momma. Shake the dreamin an think a somethin.

First thing come t'mind is Sonny. Phone's in the livin room. Gots t'call the Paradize an find out. Maybe I's better off right where I'm at. For awhile. Hunner dollahs or no hunner dollahs.

Yeah, cause if Son still got gettin up my ass in mind, I sure don't wanna go back there, specially carryin no money. That nacheral sack a twenty magic words, he'd tear my face t'pieces an take that money. An then what would I do?

Push come t'shove, maybe I can hang on here a few days.

One of the really great things about the Negro race is their sense of humor—right? They may be poor, but they don't have the worries we have. That's why they're so carefree and full of fun.

And I guess it's catching. Because going native sure did something for me. Well, you know that old saying: "The blacker the berry, the sweeter the juice."

Maybe there's something to it. Because the next day as I hurried off to the workaday world and the host of braintwisting problems awaiting me, the sight of her standing in the doorway, sort of glowing in the morning sun—well, it had me feeling so good I switched radio stations. Usually I drive to work with the Early Bird Wake-up show, but today I tuned in the "soul" station and dug it.

Now some might snicker about that. "Hire a maid one day and drive to work with so-called soul music the next day, eh. Must be very easily corrupted, that one." I can hear those narrow-minded bigots now.

But the plain fact is, I'd spent a very charming afternoon and evening getting re-acquainted with . . . Odessa. Yes, Odessa's her name now so that's what I'll call her. Sure I had sex with her. I won't deny that. I'm a normal redblooded American male, I had *plenty* of sex with her.

Not that I'm trying to cut Barbara *out*. Don't get that idea. Barbara has her life—and a very busy one it is, too—and I have mine. If I can add a maid—such a pleasurable maid to my life, what harm will that do?

I won't keep her at the beach house all the time, either. Once we have an on-going working relationship —once I've domesticated her, you know, I'll install her in my house in town. We have two bedrooms and a den. All I have to do is convert the den to a maid's room and we're all set—right? Ha! Then Barbara won't have to *put* me out on the couch for the night, I'll get out of her pincurlers and stay out.

Which reminds me: Odessa wears a *wig!* Yes, a wig. And all along I thought that was her own hair. The point is, when she takes this wig off. . . . How should I say this? Well, I mean I never knew how soft and good-smelling a colored girl's hair—her own natural hair can be. It sure beats pincurlers!

And *clean! Wow,* is she clean. Now my wife, even with all her good breeding and built-in elegance, her poise and knowledge and whatnot, some mornings when I lift the covers to get out of bed, it smells like a cesspool down there. But Odessa—she showers and washes and cleans cleans cleans. You may think Negroes have a foul body odor, but I'm here to tell you not this one—she's as fresh as a breath of spring air.

And cook—man, can she cook! With a maid like her around, I can quit throwing the same old charcoal-grilled steak parties and lay out a feed the gang will talk about for months.

On top of which, I'll be saving her from a life of crime and violence in the streets, of course. By giving her a good home. I mean a home to live in.

James Cartwright Holland, you old rascal you! Why, you've landed yourself your own island complete with native girl. Even if she is from an underprivileged background, a so-called *sub*culture, you've got a good thing going! Or you will have, as soon as she's domesticated. So ride that filly. Discipline her. Break her in. Keep the bit in her mouth till she sees stars and stripes. Oh— and don't forget you're on a mission for the inner circle.

Well, enough. I only mention the above to let you in on how I was feeling that morning as I drove to work. I'm not trying to compare those two—my emancipated wife and Odessa. In the first place, they're not even members of the same race. And secondly, Barbara has her own creative projects for the community and all, because she's such a tremendously capable woman. I mean even if she can't cook so well. Can't keep the dishes clean. Even with a dishwasher. Can't make it to the supermarket without putting a new dent in the Ford. And when she gets there, can't seem to buy what we don't have. She's just not cut out for that role. It was wrong for me not to realize this long ago. With a full-time maid, she'll be free. I won't even ask her to submit any more and she can see her psychoanalyst *twice* a week, for all I care.

Because. . . . But I won't even go into all that. I mean when it comes to the bedroom, Odessa's a pro. It's not Barbara's fault she has a few hangups. She had a horrible experience as a teenager—seduced by a child-molester at age fourteen. Which meant doctors, investigations, courtrooms, the whole ball of wax.

So you just can't compare the two—right? And the only reason I mention it is to give you an idea of my situation. As I drove to work that morning, listening to so-called soul music. Parked the car and strode into the Courthouse whistling "Dixie." Ready, willing and able to cope with whatever the day might bring.

Or so I thought. But the first thing the day brought was, a glance at my desk calendar that told me tonight is the night of the all-important Swansup function. Cocktails and dinner at the home of Samuel Swansup, financial backbone of the Party's majority faction. *And* certain-certain anti-liberal members of the opposition as well.

That brought me down a little. Gave me a headache, if you want to know the truth. Now I've got to call Odessa and tell her I won't be home till late. Maybe very late.

So, an hour after I'd left my native isle in such high spirits, I'm on the phone with bad news. Which she took philosophically enough. Said she had things to do too. Asked if I minded if she put through a call to the city and had a friend bring her a change of clothes and whatnot.

Perfectly all right by me, I assured her. After all, I said, you're not in captivity.

Then I hung up and made a mental note to buy that maid's uniform at the first opportunity, and before I'd even finished scribbling it, my wife was on the line.

What happened to me last night, she wants to know. Ha! Why hadn't I come home? Ha and ha again.

Slept at the beach house, I told her.

Why hadn't I called—she'd been worried sick about

me. She even called the police and reported me *missing!*

What? I almost blew my cool! Had to grit my teeth to keep my voice down. Told her to call the police *back*, tell them I'm *not* missing.

Do you plan to sleep at the beach house for *ever*, she wants to know.

Might not be a bad idea, now that *she* mentioned it, I say.

Well, am I aware that we have a social commitment this evening?

Indeed I am. And I'll be home this afternoon to change for it, if it's all right with her.

And that was that. It was business as usual for the next hour or so. Then Harry Hooper popped in on me.

Now Harry's usually a jovial sort, so I greeted him with, "Well well well, if it isn't the incredible Harry the Hoop! Just the man I'm looking for. What's on your mind? Gettin' much, ha ha ha?"

His response was like a slap in the face. Never cracked a smile. Leaned over my desk and in a surly near-whisper he asked me if I'd mind having a word with him.

We went across the street to the hotel for coffee, took a table off by itself, and as soon as we'd been served, Harry drills me with his famous piercing blue eyes and he says, "Now, about this nigger bitch you're shacking up with."

The trouble is, the board's inner circle doesn't let Harry in on some of our more undercover moves. I mean, because of his avowed membership in the John Birch Society, some of them think he's an extremist of sorts. Well, until we can rid their minds of that prejudice, there are certain matters we just don't mention around Harry.

107

"Do you have any idea what you're letting yourself in for?" he asks. "Do you *know* this girl? Do you know who she *is*? Have you ever heard of *blackmail*? Or were you born yesterday?"

And how could I tell him I was on a CIA-type mission, not out shacking up. All I could do was sit there and let him talk.

"This Odessa Smith character," he says, "she's nothing but a *whore*. She runs around with dope-pushers and thieves—those are her friends. She'd slit your throat as quick as look at you. She's one of the toughest prostitutes in town. She's an alley cat. Completely amoral. Not even the respectable niggers want anything to do with her. She's the very stereotype they're trying to destroy as an image."

Well, here I just had to interrupt. Tried to tell him he had the thing all wrong. That I wasn't "shacking up" —I'd hired a maid, that's all. She was in my summer place cleaning house, and when she's done there, I'll transfer her to my town house to do the cooking and cleaning, babysitting and whatnot, and one of these days I'll throw a bash and lay a feed on him he'll talk about for months.

But he only laughed, and not so good-naturedly, either. Said, "Expect me to believe *that*? Straighten out your story, Buddy boy."

Which nettled me a bit. So I said, "Harry, who the hell are you—you of all people—to bear down on me for associating with one of them? You think it's a secret about you? You and that woman on the other side of town and the family you have by her?"

"That," he says, "is different." And he went on to say, in rather rough language, that he keeps his Negro in the ghetto, and for me to take one of them out and install her in my own home—summer or winter, it made

108

no difference—that this was an act on my part that was totally against the American grain, flag and fabric.

Yes, and here's what else he said—I remember it clearly: "Buddy boy, I'm talking to you like a father. Do you realize what this can do to your oceanfront investment? Furthermore, keeping a woman in one's own home constitutes, in this state, an act of commonlaw marriage, and that makes you a bigamist. Not only are you about to ruin yourself, your property value *and* your marriage, but you're about to ruin your career. Did you know that? Because the board will be forced to take action to dismiss you from your job, Buddy boy. Unless you get that"—so-and-so black such-and-such—"the hell out of your *home*."

Obviously there'd been a horrible misunderstanding here, somewhere. I just wasn't sure where, exactly. I mean I tried to tell him that no matter what *else* is involved here, I do have the right to hire a maid—*don't I?*

But it seems he made a clear distinction in his mind between hiring a girl like Odessa to become a maid and hiring one who is already a maid. And he said, "Look, J. C., that girl's been on the phone to her friends. The word's out. It's all over town she's *living* with you. Nobody cares if you hire a *maid*. And nobody'd care if you hired *that* girl as a playmate. For one night or a dozen nights. But, Buddy boy, you do *not* take a nigger —especially a nigger like that—and go driving around like a pair of agitators. And you do *not* move her into your house. You do not do *violence* to certain sacred traditions and expect to get away with it. Not unless you're prepared to throw away your whole *life*."

Stinging words from a man such as Harry. Especially when I admire him so.

But it was only the beginning. My day went from

bad to worse. I stuck around for lunch with Harry, hoping to patch it up, and I no sooner got back to my office than I'm being ground under again! This time by our new Chairman of the Board, Herskowitz. "I'd like a few words with you, son," he says. Shoos my secretary out, locks my office door and tells me how his parents came to this wonderful country from Eastern Europe, where they'd been oppressed and persecuted. Like millions of other immigrants, he said, they found America the land of opportunity.

So he can certainly sympathize with my concern for the plight of the Negro, he said, but concern must not be allowed to degenerate into immorality and chaos. The poor have always been with us, he said, and race prejudice is as old as the Bible.

Now what is really important, he said, is for County officials like us to live lives that are above reproach, because we set the tone for the entire community and when we slip into the gutter, it brings down the entire image. Our morals, he stressed, are closely watched. We should live like we're covered with bugging devices. From morning till night, day in and day out.

I mean he behaved like he'd completely forgotten that I am on a perfectly legitimate information-gathering mission. That he himself, as a member of the inner circle, had *approved* this mission. Now why is he castigating me for carrying it out? I mean I tried to explain that all this business he objected to is necessary. How else can I learn—in any reliable way—exactly who instigated that insurrection? I've got to show her I'm concerned and want to help, because we've got to get them to stop their mounting lawlessness and solve the Negro problem. Our riot was tame compared to some, so before we have a lot of looters running wild,

I've got to get her talking honestly and freely, and all I'm trying to do is win her confidence.

But after I went through all this, he just shrugged it off. Just shrugged it off! Told me I'd been indiscreet in my *approach* to my mission, said one should never bring such a business problem *home*. No matter how important or secret it is. And in *my* case, he said, I should know better than to let myself be seen out driving around in broad daylight with a known sex offender.

I was weak when he unlocked the door and walked out. Completely shook. I almost laughed out loud when he said *sex offender*. Quite the opposite, I almost said— and I speak from experience.

Darned if I'll sit through any more of *this*, I thought. So I escaped. Knocked off for the day and went home. Where, I *hoped*, I could be alone for awhile. To relax, think, ponder all this reaction I was getting.

Because Barbara's usually out during the afternoon. Yes, and today's her art and literature group discussion. She's in the museum.

Oh yeah? I open the door from the garage to the kitchen and I'm hit by this virtual verbal whirlwind.

"Get out of my house you filthy nigger-lover. Don't you dare even touch that doorknob. You're diseased. Oh I heard about you. Heard all about it. And if you think you're ever going to sleep with *me* again, you're out of your *mind*. You're not even going to sleep in the same *house* with me. You're *insane*. You belong in an institution and I'm going to see that you're *put* in one."

Et cetera and so forth. Here she is, the very one who *told* me to go out and get myself a quote nigger bitch unquote, and now listen to her. Well, I told her a thing or two. You certainly are carrying equal rights for

111

woman a bit far, I said. Yes sir, this time you've gone *too* far.

I mean it's one thing for her to stand on her legal rights to possess our child, our home and our common property, but its something *else* for her to threaten me with *incarceration!*

I'd liked to have given her a *real* piece of my mind but what the heck. Trying to reason with the little woman—you know how that is. Sometimes you can't get a word in edgewise. All you can do is take it on the chin and ride with the punches and hope she doesn't mean everything she's saying.

Well, after about half an hour of this, I decided I'd leave. Figured I'd take what I need for the evening, drive to the beach house. Maybe there I could get some peace and quiet. So I got out some clothes—suit, tie, shirt, socks, shoes, underwear—and was on my way out of there—when I'm bashed in the ears by this screaming: "And where do you think you're going *now?* Come back here, you!"

I still didn't blow my cool—give me credit for that. I turned and I said, "But Barbara, first you tell me I'm not welcome here, then you won't let me leave! Which is it, sweetheart?"

"You'll not embarrass *me*," she screeches to the whole city. "I won't *have* it. We have an important social commitment this evening, and you'll *keep* your commitments, Mister! You'll not run out on me and make me the laughing stock of the town. Not on your life. You get right back in here. You'll put that rag back where you got it and you'll get out your *best* blacktie suit. I won't be *seen* with you in that rag, not at the Swansups. And that's where we're going, Mister. Just like nothing's happened. Do you hear me?"

Could have heard her from the other end of Main Street. And by this time, she had herself in such a state, she ran into the bedroom sobbing.

Well, come what may, a man does have his marital obligations. Both legal and moral. So in I went to do what I could to comfort her. I was even so optimistic to hope I might calm her down enough to break the good news: that I was hiring a fulltime maid so she'd be relieved from the drudgery of housework.

Trouble was, any time I got anywhere near her, she screamed like a stuck pig. Over-reacting, obviously. I went to pat her and say, "There, there, sweetie, everything's going to be all right, you'll see"—and she smacks me with, "Get your diseased nigger-loving hands *off* me, you *brute*. Don't you dare touch me."

So let's skip on to cocktail time, shall we? The baby-sitter has arrived and we've somehow managed to get dressed for the affair, and we're on our way. Though I must say it seemed like my whole world had crumbled and was lying at my feet in ruins. Worse yet, I was in such a state of shock I wasn't quite comprehending the dreadful seriousness of it all. Kept thinking: How can Barbara call Odessa *dirty?* Odessa's nothing but clean, and the least that can be said for Barbara is, she does have a problem with "feminine odors," so-called. Even if she had her Ph.D., she'd still have that!

An indication of what a state of shock I was in, as we drove to the Swansups. But you'd never have thought it, if you'd seen us—sitting there all spruced up, driving along in the Jag with dignity and poise. Pulling up the circular drive of the Swansups' massive, sprawling, immaculate grounds. Alighting as a servant took the car to park it. A Negro servant.

I've got to hand it to her, she sure can act natural,

113

my wife. Walked in that front door holding my arm, smiling, nodding, exchanging friendly greetings. The image of the Pepsi Generation sociables, that's us.

And *she* maintained that image for the entire event. It was *me* who went to pieces. After a day like I'd just had, I felt entitled to a few good stiff ones during Happy Hour—so I *thought*. But the fun wasn't over, you see. I was getting some awfully strange looks. Well, the heck with them. Tomorrow I'll think this whole business over and get my life straightened out. Somehow. Tonight I ignore them and commune with the great god Bacchus.

And that became my downfall. Because while some of them only hawk-eyed me and others avoided me like the plague, several began dogging my every step like I was a spectacular happening. Sara Wineheart came panting after me and Mrs. Hooper, of all people, leered at me like she wanted to eat me. Plus some of the ladies in that crowd who'd never given me so much as the time of day before—well, they formed a line just to flash their dentures at me. Before I knew what was going on, I was surrounded by this . . . these *ladies*. Which is when I was hit by the crowning touch—Wally Comsnot.

Five children he has and a perfectly normal wife, but . . . well, to be blunt about it, Wally's a *fag*. Queer as a three-dollar bill. It's just one of those things, I guess. I mean with Wally, you can't really hold it against him—he's not out in the streets with those longhaired Berkeley types. He's old family, you see, and . . . well, everybody's used to the idea—Wally Comsnot is a fag, and when he gets high, *look out!*

He'd never paid any attention to *me* before, but tonight—wow! Elbows his way in through this ring of ladies that's formed around me, and he really turns it on. "Thay, baby, let-th me an you cha-cha, what d'ya thay, handthome?" As he runs his wet palm down the front of my suit.

Naturally this attracted attention. Wally'd had three martinis by this time, and so had I. And, well, one thing led to another, and by the time we'd both had six, all hell broke loose. To make a long story short, I punched him. I've got nothing against him, really, and I'm not about to let a fag cause me to over-react. On the other hand, I'd had it up to *here*, by this time, so when Wally tried to drag me upstairs, I lost my head. I decked him.

Which put a bit of a damper on the party, I fear. Everybody agreed I should sober up. You just don't *hit* Wally. He's harmless, and you have to take his homosexuality for what it is, a *sickness*. Besides, he's a County official and a higher-up Party functionary.

But gosh darn it, I *knew* what he was up to, with that routine. And so did everyone else. You know that business about how any white man who goes around in broad daylight with a Negro woman—he's a latent homosexual. Well, Wally and the rest of them were using this on me. Just harmless fun, you might say, but the trouble is, I wasn't feeling like fun. Anyhow, I don't *believe* that business. Not any more. Even if it's a scientific finding, I must be an exception to the rule. I did not crave to have sex with Wally—all I wanted was to be left alone.

But enough. Overall, the party was a success. Mr. Swansup announced he's coming up with a hefty campaign contribution, and that's what we'd all come for—the Swansup money.

I didn't stay for dinner. After my to-do with Wally, Barbara took me by the arm and led me out and loaded me into the car. I was drunk as a loon by that time. She drove—in utter silence, I might add. Turned off her party charm the moment we got into the car and sat there sneering, averting her gaze and sort of communing with herself.

Pulled into the garage, got out and slammed the car door. Slammed the door to the kitchen.

Well, I had a couple of choice comments to make about that action. Which I don't think would meet with acceptance in print. As I moved over behind the wheel, because I had facts to face. Basic considerations. A very important decision to make. Besides, I had a woman waiting for me.

Round midnight I'm snoozin on the sofa an somethin wake me up. Him, standin here swayin back an forth.

I'm drunk as the lord an gonna get drunker. Bummed out a my mind! Can you mix a martini? Then go to it. One for me an one for you.

Loaded! Ooh-wee is he loaded. He sure don't need another. But I gets behind the bar an start mixin.

Throws his coat on the sofa an sinks down in the easy chair. Chin on his chest, steady starin at me, frownin.

Hmmm. I say, Hey Honey, why you lookin thataway? I do somethin t'make you unhappy?

Shakes his head like he's jes wakin up. Say, Oh no, not you. An then he start tellin me how his white friends been givin him a bad fuckinover.

Hey, here's me, I'm mixin martini, I say, Lookahere Checkerboard, don't you allow the ofay t'fuck with you. Them peoples ain't no better'n anybody else. They jes all blowed up on themselves. Thinks they own the world. Bunch a blowed up bullfrogs's all they is. Stuck straws up they assholes an got filled fulla air. Don't never let 'em think you afraid of 'em. They smells you's afraid they hop on you back an don't never get off.

Runnin my mouth till I almost tole him he oughta dig the vee-ets an watch on tee vee how they stand up t'them blowed-up bullfrogs. Beatin an killin an bomb droppin on them vee-ets for years, tryin t'put them in some kinda niggertown, but they jes ain't about t'scratch an shuffle. Showin the whole world how t'stand up t'whitie. Yeah, you sure can catch some spirit from them.

But what the hell goin on here? How is whitefolks fuckinover Jay? He jes's bright white an dead right as the rest of 'em.

I say, Bay-ba how come whitefolks be givin *you* trouble?

Stands up an walks over an looks out the winda at the ocean. Big bright moon out, waves flashin moonlight. An he say, They givin me hell because of *you!*

Well he *says* it t'the ocean. I thunk he *mean* the ocean. But then he turn on me an say, Because of *you!*

Me? What'd *I* do?

Open his mouth like he gonna run it down but nothin comed out. Spose he jes too drunk.

Okay, he wants another. I got it ready an pours it out. He carries it t'the easy chair an sinks down.

Then he tells how he went t'some party an everybody there knows he shackin up with me, an they was gamin him behind that. He say, An some *fag* propozishun me.

Oh bay-ba, I sure hopes you save some fo' me-ee.

118

Odessa, don't be silly! They're all upset because of *you!*

Hey lookahere, if they's upset cause a me, send 'em on over t'see me. Man I's in practice. Can crisscross whitie's wires till they tongue sayin jes what they ain't never spose t'let it say.

She-it, I can handle them es-oh-bees. Nine outa ten is only livin in milkywhite niggertown anyhow an scared a bein brung down t'the real black niggertown, an I been survivin in that jungle all my life, ain't got no more down t'be scared a goin.

But I don't say all that. I jes let him rattle on. Talkin how he scared a losin his job cause his boss this an his boss that.

She-eee-it. This Checkerboard so fulla scratch an shuffle I take on a pain he oughta feel. Some a these whitemens needs a boss so bad they never gets t'find out what they wants for themselves. Lookahere, they starts out with a momma-boss, goes from there to a teacher-boss, gets put in the service an gets a army-boss, comes back to a company-boss and makes it home every night to a wife-boss. No fuggin wonder they ain't ready t'be they own boss. They's hooked on boss-junk.

Humph! Talkin all this boss-junk an scared a losin his job shit, I got a good mind t'tell him t'carry my clothes down t'the car and run me back t'jail.

Yeah but the mothah'd put me out on the street, most likely. An then I'd have Sonny t'be scared of. He's scared a losin his job and I's scared a losin my face. Now ain't that some kinda a fare-thee-well.

His drink's empty again so I gets up t'mix more. Might's well let him rattle on, pour gin down him an let him gargle on it.

While I'm mixin, he quits talkin an goes t'the baffroom, an when he come back I gots his nex drink ready t'hand. An you know what? He gots a reefer. Yeah, he come out carryin a reefer.

Ole habit a mine, leavin 'em on top a the toilet, case the fuzz blow in I can flush 'em fast.

Picks the drink up an he say, Where's a match? I feel like tryin one a your cigarets.

Gets a match out an he fires up.

Ha! I hope he bees so drunk he don't know the diffrence.

Wobbles an falls back down in his chair, lickin booze from one hand, blowing pot from the other.

I can hardly keep from laughin, he lookin so wild.

Then he say, Funny taste, this cigaret.

Yeah, I say, Turkish.

Smacks his lips an he say, Hmmm. Very expensive t'bacco?

Oh yeah, five bucks a bag.

You have expensive tastes.

Um hmmm, I sure do.

This t'bacco, it's very thin, very fine.

That's right. Turkish.

Then he say, Can you tell me, Odessa? I've got to know so I can keep my job an advance myself, you unnerstand. Who started that riot?

Oh man, that's easy. Cop name Henry. I don't know his last name, we calls him Henry Brown Hound. Travels with a dog in his car an he likes boys.

But alla time I'm telling the mothah, he settin there shakin his head back an forth, no no no. An he say, No cop started that riot. Riots all over the country. *Burn*ing, *loo*ting, wagin *war*. What I wanna know is, why is the Nee Grow tryin t'kill the white man?

Hey, which Nee Grow's this that's tryin t'kill some whiteman?

The riot, the riot!

I say, Baby them cops was *white!* Any spade cops in on it, they sure don't count for brothers.

Pleeeeease! Odessa please be serious. It's important! How did that riot get started?

I tole you, a cop name Henry. He tole some teenage boy, Halt! *Luvs* this boy, you dig? That's Henry. But lookahere, this boy's in the middle a the avenue. Can't for crissake halt right there, some car liable t'run him down. So he keeps on goin, an crazy ole Henry—he been cravin this boy some time now—he musta thunk the boy was runnin from him. An he pulls out his gun an shoots across the street, kills this boy on the far sidewalk.

That cop's jes plain fixheaded. Hell, he don't gotta hit on teenage boys. Plenty brownies hangin out. One a the girls in the Paradize, Rita, she's a he. Never know it t'find her at the bar in her catchin clothes, but jes go on up with her an trick. Specially get stoned first an then go up, an you sure enuff think you's on the strongest stuff you ever-ever had, she pulls down her panties an up jump her thing. I oughta know cause she buys pussy from me now an then. First time I ever went with that broad I like t'fainted. My mind didn't stop buzzin fo' daze.

Now if Henry Brown Hound a met up with Rita, her wig off an her boys clothes on, he'd a been a cool dude. Steada out gunnin down that one boy. Anyhow behind him shootin that one, the other boys got mad. Went t'throwin stuff at ole Henry, tryin t'run him off. An that's what brung out the other robots. You know how them little chollies sticks t'gether. An directly Saterdy night they comed screamin over an shoots up the whole place, an I spose they done put it on the tee vee that we *hates* 'em.

Wa-el, he say, you do hate 'em, don't you?

Hate 'em! Man, you ever had the cops t'drive up an try killin *you*? You ain't got *time* t'love 'em.

But some Nee Grows *fought* the police, he say.

Ye-ass? Well I sure wishes it was more'n jes some.

You mean you'd fight too?

Hell yeah! Maybe holdin up flowers'll save a teeny-bopper from a split-open skull, but flowers won't keep a bullet outa my black hide. An don't give me no learn-baby-learn shit, neither—I done learned it. Them honkies come on like some kinda mad dogs an the onlyest thing even slow 'em down is shoot back. Looka-here, I knows they's nothin but overseers on the big plantation, jes doin like Big Charlie tell 'em to. But that don't cut nothin when I can't get nowhere near Big Charlie—all I got left t'do is kill them little chollies he send over t'kill me. Yeah, an that's what all the colored peoples all over the world gonna be doin, one a these days. Rise up t'gether an shoot back at them little cholly mad dogs, an you better know it too.

All the aitch bombs Big Charlie got ain't gonna help him. The stronger them bombs, the weaker his hoodoo, an the world's round, baby—sooner or later he gonna meet it all comin back around t'get him. Chickens comin home t'roost.

Well you oughta seen Jay's face when I'm done rappin on that. Lookin at me like I done name the end a the world. Ha! *His* world, yeah.

Goes t'say somethin but he been steady pullin on that reefer till it done caught up. Don't spose he never had a smoke like that before, huh. An now he got two things trippin him out. Open his mouth t'talk an all he get out is, O . . . Dessa . . . you got a dis . . . a dis . . . a dis. . . .

I gots a *what*?

All he can do is keep shakin his head no.

She-it. I get up an pick the glass out his hand, pour him another. This time I gots t'curl his fingers round the glass, he so stoned.

You gonna be ready fo' bed soon, Jay?

No! Wanna talk. Talk, wanna talk. Bout the . . . ry-yet!

Sweeheart, that riot'll keep till mornin. You looks like you needs some sleep. Come on, drink up an finish yo' cigaret an let's make it t'bed.

Ha! That smoke sure put him away. Man, he's all wound down t'nothin but *sighs*. Breathin in, sighin out. Takes one last swallow a his martini an then I puts myself in his way, leads him inta the bedroom.

Floomps down on that bed, fallin-down tired.

Jay, I say, roll over, let me take off yo' clothes.

But I gots t'do the rollin for him. All he can do is mumble bout how he ain't had nothin t'eat since leven o'clock.

Um mm, sweetheart, no wonder you's stoned. Go straight t'sleep now. T'morra momma gonna make you a breakfes'll bring you right back t'the land a the livin. Yeah, you jes go t'sleep thinkin how good that gonna taste.

He's out like a light fore I even get it all sed. Now I gots t'*wrench* them covers. He layin on top of 'em. An I had t'go an play *made* this afternoon!

Well I wrench an wrench an finely get him unner them covers. Onlyest reason I made the bed is my friends come down t'day. Yeah, ten of 'em. Drove down in four cars. Brung me my clothes an records an my stash a pills.

Had a hell of a time tellin 'em where this place is at. Call Jane at the hotel an she was layin up with Couzin Joe, an when I try t'tell him, he sharptalks me. Says,

I ain't no crystal ball. You find out the name a that road you's on an call me back.

Sure did worry me, not knowing where I's at. But pretty soon Jay Checkerboard calls an tells it that he ain't comin home till late. Ax him the name an he say I's on the ole bay road.

Calls Joe back an direckly here come four sheens fulla holes an hozes. What we calls 'em, crowd I hangs out with.

Hey you oughta seen all them peoples when they sets eyes on where I'm at. Come out them cars all callin me missy suburb housewife. An me, I stooded up on the top step holdin a broom, runnin my mouth, talkin shit t'Jane—I's gonna beat yo' blackass down t'blowed out blue, yo' don't carry my rags t'the washhouse an bust yo back scrubbin—wha's at yo' say bitz?—don't yo' mumble at me, hoe—lissen heah, yo' shuffle yo' feets an grin Aunt Jemima—bring my clothes back from the washhouse flashin like the white knight hit 'em, you heah?

An here they all come trompin up them steps, pile up here in the livinroom. Weight down this house till I worry for the house-legs.

Joe, he say, Odessa you sure enuff be droppin some wild combinashuns. Where you get the pills you's on? Jail? Girl I *know* you bees dreamin all this up. I *gots* t'be peekin in on some dream you's havin.

Funny thing, huh. That dream last night.

Well I say, *Dreamin!* What chew talkin bout, dreamin! Man, I'm layin up with Caukaishun hair ticklin my thighs.

Mess around this house for awhile, talkin shit. They tells me how Sonny still out there holdin up the hotel, waitin on me. An how Son runned a game on Jay Checkerboard. Yeah, couple nights ago Jay come over an was trompin up them bandid houses an Son copped over fifty off him. Got high an some a them other hypes beat him for the rest, so then he went chippying with Big Dot an the first time she turn her back, he lightened up her purse.

Ha! I say, Dot you got jes the kinda trickin you was askin for, chippying with my ole man. You dum bitz, you think he was cravin pussy? Ha!—you sure did learn.

Took eight dollahs off Dot. Got high again, got beat for the rest by the other hypes again, an the last they seen he was back out holdin up the hotel, layin for my blackass.

One a them hozes, Zeek, he say, Odessa yo' oughta see him. Looks like some kinda Danyal Boon huntin nacheral female coon.

An I tole all them holes an hozes, I say, Go on back an tell that man I's all squared up an so far off the corner he ain't never ever gonna know where t'look. Tell him he gonna be nothin but skull an bones time I get back. Gonna be a *skellington* holdin up that hotel.

An when we was all talked out, we pops reds an leave our shoes in the house, an we goes boogalooin barefoot down the beach. Two tranzizters goin, everybody struttin, havin a celebrashun.

Last girl t'make it off the corner was Lola, an her ole man throwed a party. Way up in this partment they got downtown. Yeah, an that was a big-big party sure enuff.

But she-it, I ain't really off the corner like Lola was. I ever do get off, I sure ain't gonna mess up like she done. Couldn't keep her twoit off new stuff. Comed back t'the Paradize every chance she got an freaked off with everybody.

Her man—we all call him Bigdaddy—he didn't mind

that so much, cause he like t'party himself. But when he come home an found her in his own bed ballin his very best friend, he drew the line. Nex time we seen Lola she was all done. Both eyes shut an all bloodied up from being kicked through a glass door. Pushed her out a car an left her layin in the street fronta the hotel, an now all she ever hussle is eggs.

Anyhow, my friends don't go till late this affernoon. An Joe, he say, Hey Odessa, ain't you never comin back an see us no more? You gone highass?

Yeah, I tole 'em, I sure is. Gonna keep on highass till Sonny give up tryin t'get up my ass. Till he give up an find himself some new thing. I say, But y'all come down here an see me. Look in on this hole sister now an then. My man goes t'work every mornin an I's here all alone. An lissen heah, y'all gots t'keep up my stash. Supermarket sure don't sell no grass.

Everybody knows I ain't really no missy suburb housewife but it's a kick makin believe. Well if ole Jay Checkerboard was jes a little blacker—but he so deep deep white I ain't nowhere with him.

Sittin in the livinroom recallin all this, lissenin t'Jay snore. An I thinks a what he tole me yestiday when he was drivin me here. Ko-operate, save, experiment. An I lays back my head an tells it t'the smoke I'm blowin, I say, What goes out around come back around, so whatever he bees t'me I's gonna double it up back t'him.

Well he got me in a nice house, that's a stone sure certain. Yeah, so t'morra what I better do, better give him some real good womantendin. Breakfes', lovin. Keep steady re-activatin him, get him movin on past whatever took his jump.

Hey, Joe was jivin t'day, he say, Oh missy suburb housewife, can I be yo' lawnboy? Trim yo' pearltongue? An I tole him my new man trim me good, I don't need no lawnboy.

Knowed I was jes jivin back but it sure be a gas if I did get ole Jay ofay so fulla jump he was t'be really mellow back. Ha! I sure could take care a that man nice if he was ready for it. Yeah, an if he got tired a me alla time, I'd jes fetch a couple dollies from the Paradize, put him through a spring change-up, get him lively again.

Sittin here thinkin this an lookin over my stash a pills an stuff, an I notice those four white longies. Um mm, I sure glad my friends brung these.

Gots a real mellow trick makes these longies. Tole me when he give me these four, tole me don't drop but one at a time an don't for crissake play combinashuns.

Trippin'est pills I ever put down. Ooh, these is the hope-t'die Mahstah trippers, all ways. First time I ever drop one, that little mothah run me through the most wildest changes—I mean t'tell it like it is, that trip broke my ole self down an put me back t'gether brand-baby-new.

Wonder could I take Jay trippin with me? I'm sure gonna go. Do me good t'blow my mind an clean out my soul. Yeah an he sure could stand a blowin out, too. That's a stone sure certain.

Gag zoots!

Gad *zooks*, what a mess I'm in. One night with Odessa and it's like an earthquake hit my whole life. Suddenly all the underpinnings of who and what I am are in danger of collapse. Career, property, marriage—my very image in the community.

That's what was racing through my mind as I drove to the beach house. I had to do something but I hated to face just what that something should be. Must I get rid of her to save my own skin?

Well, when I got there, the first move she made was a pipe-and-slippers routine, sort of. Softened me up, I'll admit. I might even go so far as to say that wives should be more like her.

Oh God! That's not what I mean at all. I'm not trying to poo-poo wives and say they should be Negro prostitutes—what I'm trying to convey is that the few nights I've gone out on the town and come home tanked up and a bit wobbly on my legs, my wife immediately offers some not so gentle value judgments. Whereas Odessa, who was snoozing on the couch when I arrived, sleeping with such a sweet, innocent, child-like look of wonder on her face, woke up smiling and all ready to fix a nightcap and hear my sad tale.

Which is why, I guess, I didn't just tell her right off that tomorrow she'd have to go back where she came from. Because this experiment can't work, I guess. Owing to difficulties completely beyond control.

Well, I just didn't have the heart and the next thing I knew I was settled back with a nightcap, observing how she'd cleaned the place to a spic 'n' span shine. Ah ha, I thought, she *is* accepting her responsibilities as a maid after all.

But that realization only complicated my inner conflict. Tore me to pieces inside. While at the same time I was feeling so much "at home," I must have looked very much at ease. Very comfortable. Completely relaxed.

And it was a relief not to have to face a wife who is either going to judge me or challenge me or go self-consciously silent. It was such a relief I ended up confiding in her. Told her all about how my friends and associates had really put me through the mill at that party, how my job was threatened, my career, my home, everything—and all because of her.

She heard me out with a sympathetic ear. Then, since there was nothing either one of us could do about *that*, I went on to the subject of the insurrection. I asked her point-blank *who* instigated that uprising.

I tend to believe she used her dialect as a hiding place, so to speak. Because half of what she said was lost in obscurantism. I mean she simply resorted to the most esoteric jargon imaginable, and chattered away at a great rate.

129

On the other hand, to be fair about it, I'd drunk enough by this time to sink a battleship. On top of which, I'd smoked one of her rare Turkish cigarettes. I'd given up smoking months ago, you see, but she had these very rare and aromatic foreign ones which you have to roll yourself, and she kept them on the back of the john, of all places. So when I went in there to "walk my dog," you know, I picked one up and decided to try it.

Well, it inhaled easily enough, but *wow*, was it strong. Man, cigars have nothing on those little Turkish items. No wonder the makings cost five dollars a pack. A real hairy-chested he-man smoke, baby.

Anyway, by the time I'd finished it, I was *whoozie*. Hadn't eaten since lunch with Harry the Hoop and I'd lost count of how many drinks I'd had, and none of these factors were an aid to communications.

So all I remember about what she said was some weird story about some policeman named Henry shooting a teenage boy, and the boy's friends throwing rocks at the policeman and that's what started the riot. Which is a lot of nonsense. I know. Remember the case very well, and it had nothing to do with that insurrection.

A boy was shot, you see, but the peace officer in question acted in line of duty. The case involved a robbery suspect who was trying to flee and the officer repeatedly ordered him to halt before acting. Furthermore, the officer never intended to kill the lad, he was only trying to wing him, and all this is absolutely documented in our police files.

But according to the warped and distorted version of it Odessa had picked up from her rumor mill, this police officer wanted to recruit this boy for the Brownies. Who are girls, not boys, and a teenager is too old for the Brownies anyway. Besides, it's not the duty of a peace officer to recruit Brownies—the Girl Scouts take good care of that.

And I'd have certainly straightened her out about that little incident, if I hadn't been so dog-tired by that time. Could barely keep my eyes open. All those martinis—by this time, I'm afraid, I was zonked! Smashed! Bombed!

Don't have the slightest idea how I managed to make it to bed. All I do remember is this frightening nightmare. In which the same thing happened to me that happened to another white man who went off to live with a colored girl.

In that other case, the guy was an engineer fresh out of college. Came to work for the County Roads Department and pretty soon the word went around that he's living with a Negro. No howling mobs, nothing like that, but he did keep getting his tires slashed and windows broken, and of course he wasn't exactly popular around the Courthouse. Finally, the police picked the pair of them up for dope. Marijuana. Hauled them off to jail and that's the last anyone ever heard about it.

Well, in this dream I had that night, *I* was being raided by the police and they were digging up all sorts of illegal dope in this very beach house. Dope and pornography. I kept telling them I had no idea where this stuff came from—and why should I be a user of illegal narcotics anyhow? I have this perfectly beautiful bar, fully stocked. And as for the pornography, I assured them that as a County official I'm a smut-hunter, not a pornographer—that's why I do, yes, have in my possession some certain-certain items, confiscated by our duly established authorities. But they wouldn't listen to me and were dragging me out bodily when I woke up.

131

To find Odessa shaking me, asking what's the trouble. I told her about the dream and she was silent for a time, then she asked, what if that cigarette I'd smoked was *weed?*

Which is a nickname for marijuana, you know, and it hit me like a jolt of electricity. Sat bolt upright in bed! Would probably have got up and thrown those things into the ocean—just in case she *wasn't* joking— except for, *ouch!* A stabbing pain shot through my head.

What a hangover! Oh, was it a lu-lu. All I could do was lie back down in bed and suffer.

Well, the next thing I know, she's standing there with a pill and a glass of water. I asked her what the name of this pill is and she said she didn't know. All she knew was it's for hangovers. I insisted she tell me the name—find the package and let me see for myself— but she said she keeps all her pills in one bottle. Said this is a green hangover pill compared to red ones and yellow ones.

I was in no condition to debate on *that* level. And it was a legitimate pharmaceutical type of pill, so I gave in and took it.

I guess it was just a sleeping pill, after all, because the next thing I know, it's 10 o'clock the next morning, and here comes my pretty little maid, carrying my electric toothbrush and a cup of coffee. Said she thought I'd like to give my teeth a "preliminary" so the coffee would taste better. So I did, and here she comes again, this time carrying rolls and honey.

It certainly isn't going to be easy to fire a maid like this, I thought. And why should I, anyhow? Nuts! I think I'll find out her vital statistics—social security number, etc.—and take out papers on her.

Suffice it to say that this idea met with an incredible obstacle. She *has* no social security number. She files no income tax return, she probably isn't listed with the census takers. She isn't even listed with the Welfare people. I mean it's like she doesn't *exist*. She doesn't have paper number one. All she has is identification cards that are admittedly phoney and unauthorized.

And while my mind was wrestling with that incredibility, the phone rang. My wife. And with Odessa's soul records playing loudly in the background, dear Barbara didn't have so much to say. Asked me what I was doing and I told her goofing off and she hung up.

Then I put in a quick call to my secretary, to tell her the obvious—that I'm not coming in today. I mean by this time it's almost noon, you see. Well, we'd had a busy morning. In bed.

Now breakfast was awaiting me. Our "main" breakfast. What the "preliminaries" had led to. And it certainly was worthy of the title "main." An omelet full of diced this-and-thats, very delicious, and a stack of pancakes that would do the International House of Pancakes proud.

What's a lady of the night doing cooking such delicious food, I quipped. To which she replied—quite seriously—she's a woman *first*.

Which somehow reminded me that today was my day to make some hard decisions, to do some deep thinking. So I told her this and she went scurrying off and came back holding up two small capsules. These, she gleefully informed me, were "think" pills. And today was her day to take one—if I wanted to take one with her, she'd be happy to quote take me with her, unquote.

J. C. baby, I said to myself. Quit kidding yourself,

this woman's got too many pills for *all* of them to be non-narcotics. That dream you had last night must have been some sort of prophecy.

"What is the name of *this* one?" I said.

Which drew a blank. She told me a *client,* so to speak, had given her these pills, to be used upon rare occasions for some deep and powerful thinking.

I'll bet! I'll just bet. "What's inside them—heroin?"

Oh no, she said, and even acted shocked that I should think such a thought. And when I asked her if they are habit-forming, she said, "Naw! Ah takes them all the time."

Well, that was the tipoff, of course. But she went on to call this pill a "rocket ship to Heaven" and put on a long song and dance about what wonderful things happen to one who has taken this pill.

What the heck, I thought, just *once* won't make me an addict, will it? And you've got to experience something before you really know what it's all about—right? And you owe it to yourself to know what's happening in the other world, the world of narcotics and whatnot.

So I took it. Downed it with coffee and watched her do the same. Who knows? Maybe it *is* some kind of "think" pill.

Anyhow, if I'm ever going to gain her confidence so she'll tell me who *really* instigated that riot, I'd better act like I trust her. And it's a beautiful day. Sun streaming in the window, so pleasant having her around. Might as well just give up and let it happen. It's *in* me now, whatever it is. So I might as well sit back and find out *what* it is.

Next day he's fulla queshuns, steady pumpin me. Wants t'know my soshal security number. I say, My *what?*

Don't you got a soshal security number?

Must be number one, ain't never had it before.

No no, can't be number one. How bout income tax. You file income tax, doncha?

Are you kiddin!

My god! No income tax statemin? How bout the sensus—they count you on the sensus?

Not unless they done it when I wasn't lookin.

Well, he say, you on welfare?

Wished I was. Welfare money don't come t'much but I could get my chittlins with it.

Don't you have any *papers?*

So I dug out my purse an shows my cards. Cost me three bills for this man t'make 'em out so's I can wear my new name.

An when he done pumpin me bout papers, he starts on havin chillrens. Yeah, coulda knocked me over with a feather when he got t'that. Say, You ever think a havin chillren?

Took a gulp a coffee an I say, Hell yeah, an I'd a had me a couple by now, I only had some place t'keep 'em.

Even in *your* life?

Sure! Lots a girls in the life has chillrens. All you need is somebody t'stop by an notice 'em now an then while you out makin it. Me, I got t'get myself built up at the hotel so's I can afford a partment. Then I gots t'find a stay-at-home somebody t'notice the babies. An most the peoples I knows is in the life, out scratchin an hoein the streets.

Leans back in his chair, looks out the winda. Wouldn't it be somethin if we had chillren?—that's him.

Okay, I'll play along. I say, Place like this we could have three, four. Half a dozen.

Gives me a funny look, an I ain't sure what he comin round to now, so I jes go on with the game. Ain't nothin t'stop us. You's a man an I's a woman. I been hoein but I kep dockterin. Doc say I's a healthy hole. All I need is a man with a hussle a his own so's when I'm laid up havin 'em, somebody makin rent.

You wanna have chillren?

Sure I do. I's a woman!

Laugh, an he say, Boy wouldn't that be somethin. Me an you havin babies. Wonder if we could get away with it.

Get away with it! Long's somebody bringin in money we's away with it. You got one an you's away with it, ain't you?

Oh, he say, he spose so. But him an his wife ain't happy.

Well I sorta knowed that, somehow. But what he sayin now sure do sound like that woman's the oh-riginal real righteous dudie on red rubber wheels.

Now ain't that a bitch. Him sufferin behind his ole lady an me needin a man. He wasn't so godam ofay I'd lay my mojo on, have us bouncin with the world come Fridy.

What a gas! I was kiddin them holes an hozes bout how I'm all squared up here, an now this man talkin babies. Ha! Whew! I's as close t'square as his red hair. A bunch a blue-eyed spade house apes inta the bargain. Hey that sure would fuck some minds, huh.

Recalls t'me that little girl I slep with Saterdy night. Man, if I was t'square up here, I could go back an get that girl an bring her here—jes t'get us goin, like. Love her up, feed her good, allow her t'come along her own way. Outside that nigger hell an away from little cholly robot an his head-smashin.

With a man like *this?* Ooh-wee, Momma, is you blowin you *wig?*

This man ain't nowhere near t'gether. Like that dream he had last night. Long about first light he woked me up sayin, Ooh, ummm, no no no! Let me go! Stop! Don't!

Woked him up an I ax him what's happenin? Sweatin, teeth chatterin. Tole me he dream the narks come in an bust him for possessin.

You dig it? Knows that was weed he was smokin fore he pass out but his head ain't gonna allow no such a thing from his heart. Well I ax him, jes t'make sure. I say, Spose that was weed you was smokin?

You shoulda seed it—come up in bed like I fired a gun. Then he go, *Ouch!* Ooh! Put a hand t'this head, falls back down.

Hungover. So I fish in my stash, gets out a pill an runs a glass a water, carries it to him.

Wants t'know what's *in* this pill. Say, An wha's the name?

She-it, I ain't gonna tell. He wouldn't unnerstand. So I say, Baby this pill real good for hangovers. Sometimes I'm out partyin an I gots t'pour down booze t'turn the trick, an time I gets back t'my room again my head's *splinchin!* Drop one a these, wake up the next day good's new.

I get it down him an he sleeps good. Been up two, three hours fore he come awake. Got coffee made, brekfes set t'go.

Carries in his lectrick toothbrush an a cup a coffee, an a little preliminary—biscits an honey.

Then when he sure he gonna live through it, I gets back in bed an takes us through some fun. Best way t'start a good day, nice lazy lovin in the mornin.

Goin over all this in my mind. Next peep outa him, he lean back in his kitchen chair an he say, Gotta do some hard thinkin t'day, Odessa.

An my longies come t'mind. I say, Hey I gots jes the ticket.

Run, fetch a couple, hand him one.

What's *this?*

Ain't gonna tell him the name a these neither. Um-mm, no. They got it on the tee vee an radio that this here pill's bad, an Jay so dum he sure t'believe that tee vee hoodoo. Say, I don't know the right name—I call 'em love poshun number one hunner billyun.

I don't need no *love* poshun, I need t'*think.*

Oh it'll get you thinkin. Lissen heah, you'll think deeper on this here pill, deeper'n you ever knowed you can.

Curlin his lip.

Well I ain't gonna sit here chawin, gonna drop mine's.

Pertend t'pop it but I palm it. Then I take some coffee an set back like I sure enuff done drop the mothah.

An he drops his. For real. I seen it. Settin on his tongue an he put some coffee down behind it.

Gots t'get him through his takeoff. Yeah, cause this Mahstah sure can *zoom.*

Lookahere, first time I trip out on this, I was with the man makes 'em, an I swear t'god an allah both I thunked I was never gonna come about. I mean this shit tears you right down t'nothin but screamin funny shapes an sizes. Hypes yo' mind till you's suckin yo' thumb an cryin for yo' momma. But when you come back t'gether on it, you sure do turnout with a fine new eye on life. I mean t'say it like it is, you turnout soul peoples with everything an everybody.

Yeah an the trick makes 'em, he taught me the way t'have a real good trip is take off expectin. Like you know how sometimes when you expectin the worst, the worst happen. Expectin the best, the best happen. He say, On this here pill you gots t'take off like you's on a rocketship t'heaven—whatever heaven you wanna go.

Well I let a little time go by then I ax him t'dig out his favorite records. Put 'em on, an wait.

Direckly he say, My life's so *empty!* I'm nothin but a empty shell.

He's holdin a seashell.

Oh, I say. Look deep inside that shell, baby, an see can you find what you *really* is.

Lets more time go by, an when I hears him groan I know he's trippin for a certain. I say, Can you talk t'the ocean yet?

Jes groanin.

I say, That's okay, jes go with it. Don't feel scared if you start breakin down. Futher down you goes, the futher up you gonna come later.

Groans some more. I say, Pretty soon you gonna be diggin it all, baby. Lissen heah, first time I took one I was out in the country an I spent half the day talkin t'flowers an trees, birds an all.

Then all of a certain he lean his face up close t'mine's an say, You're every color in the rainbow.

Sure enuff?

You're not black an I'm not white. We're both . . . all . . . all colors.

Well he's flyin now. Goes over an looks out the winda an he say, I'm a *fish*. I shine in the dark. At night I'm a sun out in the vast vast . . . see.

Then he come outa that an he sits down in his big chair, takes t'starin at the floor.

Guess he's okay now, so I drops mine's for real.

Then he starts moanin an groanin somethin pityful. On his hands an knees goin through some big-big changes. Looks around an he say, Don't put my body in a air-tight casket—I wanna new *start* in life.

Looks like his trip gonna take him down fore it bring him up. That's okay, long's he don't get in no rut down there. All I gots t'do is pick him out the ruts now an then an he gonna come around fine. So I hunt for somethin t'put in his hand, somethin alive.

Ain't nothin but that seashell. An food—I opens the coffee can an pours some on a saucer, put that in his way. Say, Lookahere Jay, take a good long look at these.

But he won't. Gotta workout on somethin else first. Talkin weird dream stuff.

Go with it, baby. I's right with ya. Jes let ole Mahstah pill carry you any place. Remember what I say—the more down now, the futher up later. Get set for some sweet-sweet flyin—everythin gonna turn out so pretty you gonna tingle an sing.

Then mine's starts t'take a hold. Room's changin shape. An I can feel him sorta followin me along. Like I's holdin his hand an we's a couple a chillrens, playmates goin off t'the woods t'gether an he hangin onta my hand cause he ain't never been in these woods before.

It was like having a weird technicolored dream you can't wake up from. And *wow*, was it scary! The real world of physical things just seemed to melt and dissolve away, and here were a thousand hairy monsters driving me, like chasing me down into this nightmare. Demons. Devils. Never saw them before but . . . like, I recognized them instantly.

Well, they sort of drove me to some far-out corner, some lower depth of this nightmare and then I . . . well I just turned around and started back up. As if now that I was here, I decided it was impossible to get chased any further, so I might as well relax. And find out where to from here.

That's when it began to feel like I was going up this endless spiral stairway. Like the one I'd gone up a few nights ago in that condemned house, except that this time there were terrors so real I could *feel* them. Against my skin. *In* my skin. Their teeth, their breaths.

Frightening creatures screaming out of some nightmare forest the other side of possible. Dragons, dinosaurs, alligators, snakes, snakes and more snakes. Snarling, clutching for me with claws, biting, wrapping around me trying to kill me, eat me, claw me to bits. And I'm fighting, fighting my way up in this mad panic to escape. Through this ooze that's cascading down. A torrent of slime like a huge waterfall rushing against me.

Well, I keep pressing on and up because I know, somehow, that I'm *dead*. I see myself dead. And the only way back to life and out of this mess is to survive this torrent of slime and fight off all these nightmare monsters that are at me like some kind of vultures.

And then I got around to wondering, what is all this horror? Snakes, reptiles? But *no!*—they'd changed. Now it was like being in a tight, dense forest. A forest of houses shaped like skulls. Then it was a forest of slimy, hideous aspects. Like ghosts. But what is *this?*

And as if to answer this, I suddenly found it was *myself. I* was this menacing forest of slimy monsters that were trying to consume me. And now I was laughing at how frightened the other *I* was of this me that was threatening him. Because as soon as I saw myself as part of that mess of monsters, I had no reason to be scared. My situation seemed ridiculous.

Then Odessa walked by me and her skin had a luminous, glowing quality that seemed to draw me in, envelop me. I gave in to being absorbed and I felt good, sweet. And then I became her as a child.

And then I was scared all over again. And tense. A great ghastly image of some all-time villain loomed up like a host of faces, all leering, snarling, sadistic. I was on a street as a small black girl and a lot of white faces were peering at me, smiling. But I was afraid of them. Terrified. Knew I had reason to be. Their ugly and menacing teeth. Small and yellow and hungry to sink into my skin like knives. And I kept wondering, what is *wrong* with these people? They smile with such cruelty. Why won't they let me love? Why are they trying to block my love?

And now this mess of ghostly white faces was swarming all around me with their eerie smiles and I was reaching out trying to love them but their smiles were suffocating my love. Suddenly I realized I'd been struggling like fury to survive their hate. And their smiles, it came to me, were false. Were they trying to love? But the only force coming out of them was a strange, smiling hate.

Ah, I said to myself, they feel guilty. But instead of facing this in themselves, they're smiling these weird smiles at me. They've transferred their guilt to hate. They can't love me back. Can't let me love them—they hate themselves too much for that. All they can do is smother me with these awful smilings.

Yet in that mess of weird white faces there seemed to be a few who could love—because here I was as her again, and I was meeting *me!* I mean I was her as J. C. Holland walked in the door of that cathouse, and my heart was telling me that here was someone (J.C.) I could respond to—but he was afraid of *me*. Or of the feelings he had for me. Yes, because he had love in him but was afraid of it. And his fear was short-circuiting the current of his love.

Then I saw his love as a liquid. Stagnating, souring. Would soon turn to foul-smelling self-loathing. Like some kind of lagoon behind a fog, a swamp of pride. I saw all this so clearly I could smell the stench of the swamp. Was standing in the middle of this scene wondering, why has he dammed up this beautiful lagoon?

Why doesn't he let it ebb and flow? Like it wants to, this ocean of love. What's he so afraid of?

And it came to me that he was afraid of facing the ugly smilings within me, all that self-hate that was suffocating me. Yes, he was afraid to separate himself from that force of hate. And I felt disgusted with him, angry. And also somehow sorry for him. And then, before these feelings had subsided, I'd become her as a young woman meeting me again.

This time he (me) is trying frantically to smile his way into this force of hate, and it makes me sick to see it. I want to yell to him, Wait, stop! You're going the wrong way! You're going to some *final* death! Poisoned. You won't be able to escape into new forms of life!

But before I could even try to stop him, something was dying heavily on top of *me*. Pennypacker. He was squashing me, and he was much more than just his physical self. He was a whole mess of sights and sounds. Political rallies with rebel yells, a huge IBM machine punching holes clear through me. A wild charge of police cars with their lights blinking in a mad blaze of colors, sirens screaming like booming classical music, all coming at me at tremendous speed, trying to smash me. But I float above it all at the last instant and their blinding chrome goes roaring away beneath me.

But now Pennypacker has become a mountain of books. Law books, encyclopedias, dramatic histories of some kind of obscene something that this Pennypacker creature thinks is heroism. And here's a big fleet of fifteenth century ships being blown by some kind of, like, mental disease. Sailing off to where I now am. And here are scenes of black and brown people, Indians and Africans being slaughtered in some hot-blooded

145

technicolored orgy. And out of all this I seem to emerge in a crowd that is being whipped and put in chains. I'm a slave, a black slave, part of a mass of blacks and we are barely half alive. Now we're being forced to work in hot fields, now in steamy factories. Gradually we go from black to brown to lighter shades, and now we are every shade from ebony black to albino white, and we are climbing up this tremendous mountain of books. Climbing in a dreary darkness toward a skylight of some kind. A sun, an opening, and I am climbing as her.

Then suddenly I am face to face with J. C. Holland again and this time his fear is a quieter, more subtle feeling, and I know why—because it's occurred to me that if he, I, killed me, her, it would be a bright beginning and commencement for her, and it would be the real and absolute end of me, him. I know this because I watch him die and I sit back and observe how the bright, tiny seeds of his substance are filled with poison, and he's unable to merge with the other forms of life. He desperately wants to become the stem of a flower but the flower seed won't accept his substance. Nothing in all creation will accept his substance, the white race me. Nothing wants to admit this poison. These poisoned bits of me struggle to get in, but the other things, like cells or molecules all silently rebuff them. Lock them out in some frozen waste and they wither and die, completely.

And then I'm back as her again. I'm saying to me, Don't you see what will happen to you if you don't unblock that stagnant lagoon? Get rid of all that poison! If you want your death to be a beginning, merge your substance with mine, absorb my love and let it overpower your fear. Let me cure you, us, and then we'll die for a beginning together.

146

And I watch this happen—how love is like a sun that warms us both and makes us happy together. We sit here in this livingroom in rocking chairs, side by side, gazing out at the sea. We have children and they have children, and we look at the sea like it's a new beginning for our children—our death—and it's waiting for us and we're just sort of taking our good old time about going to it. Because we like each other as we are—even though we're both very old now and all wrinkled and infirm, we're comfortable with each other and feel accomplished. And we're just savoring this comforting accomplishment, like the last sip of a very satisfying drink. We are this drink, both of us become this sweet drink in the bottom of a fine crystal glass that sparkles like the rippled surface of the sea. It's awesome, beautiful. Everything fills us with a strange and wonderful music that seems to vibrate in us like we're its instrument.

Then I realized I was somehow ahead of myself. I separated from being us. The music subsided and was gone, and I got up from the floor of the livingroom, went down the steps and onto the beach.

Now the wind hits me. Feels like a cool shower of magic water. And it talks to me, sings to me, plays with me like a crowd of happy children all full of delight and sweet tickling sensations. I turn to it and it seems to strip me naked and make love to me, like a million playful fingers caressing my whole body, thrilling me through and through. Caresses and soothes me, draws me in, and in one blindingly wonderful moment seems to bring my delight to a tremendous intensity, like an orgasm. And I'm filled with tears of joy.

Then I was standing there all emptied out, wondering what happened a moment ago. And it occurred to me that I'd had a form of sex with the wind. One part of my mind was saying, That's the silliest thing I ever

147

heard of. But then, from somewhere else in my mind, the idea struck that sex is the common denominator of life, the essence of life, and that life was telling me this through the wind. And I suddenly wondered, Why be afraid of life? Stark naked life—it's awesome, it's a funhouse, a horrorhouse, all sensational extremes, but why *fear* it? Because I knew in a flash that even though life can be as terrifying as it can be beautiful, it's pointless to fear it. The only thing to really fear is the fear of life.

And I understood now that I'd been a fearer of life, and it felt like I was now being driven straight into the guts of this fear and on through it. And I seemed to know that once I get past a certain barrier, everything will be glorious.

And I thanked the wind, spread my arms to it, bowed to it, caressed it, and I had this magnificent sensation of *being* the wind, *feeling* the pleasure of my own gratitude.

Then suddenly she was at my side. She was saying something, without actually speaking it. She was saying, You're going along so well I want to go with you. Come on, let's walk on the beach.

So I go with her—or she with me—and the sand under our feet, now I'm feeling her feet as my own and mine as hers, and this sand is the distillation of all the sparkling moments of sex and ecstasy that ever were, in the lives of any who ever were. And they're telling us through our feet, each grain of sand, telling of this ecstasy. They're speaking from centuries ago, it seems. From eons and other worlds. Yet time doesn't exist. Oceans and oceans of time from far galaxies of the past are the present moment, and this moment is always, eternity. Our feet listen to these grains of sand, feel their joy with them, and I'm overwhelmed with love. For everything. For her and for each grain of sand that is the ecstasy of everyone, and there seems to be no more distinction between the sand and my own overwhelming love.

And it came to me that loving her I was loving everyone. Every *thing*.

Now my whole body was singing with love. Singing and singing like the wind, caressing her, making love to every inch of her, every sweet pore in her skin, every heartbeat, all the flow of all her blood and fluids, every crease and crevice of her, and her whole being was singing with my singing love. And the wind was making love with us, to us, and the waves of the sea were frolicking in overcome with joy to see us all making such wonderful love. I was so filled with love I felt like I'd fly apart and become the wind and sea, and sand and sky. I couldn't contain my *self!* The only way I stayed put together was by becoming her again, because as her I felt a cooler, quieter love, a love I could live with.

And that's when this drug began to wear off. I was standing with her, seeing her as herself—I was entirely me again—and she was saying, You've been tripping real good, baby. But it was like the sound of her voice was coming from her eyes. And it was so wildly absurd that I slipped back for just a moment to see myself as her again, and I heard my own black self say it. Now I was both of us and she was as much me as I am, and we were together in some sweet indescribable loveplay with everything around us. Sea, wind, sand, sky—the blue of the sky was showering its delight on us and those big delicious clouds were puffed with pleasure for us. I put my arms around her lightly and I held the whole sky. Was in love with the sky, nibbled at those big, clean, lovely clouds, and they all—everything—whispered delight.

Then without words she was saying, Let's go back to the house. And I thought of that Spanish saying, *Mi casa, su casa*. Understanding of it came to me, and I knew she understood that I understood it, and everything was so glistening and absolutely beautiful, so sparkling and radiating loveliness I just have no words to say it.

Hangs onta me a long time. Slows me down. Like mines jes startin t'take ahold an he say, I'm *black!* Odessa I become *you!* Ooh! Oh! Life's fulla white enemies.

What's he doin? Coppin my trip? Feel like tellin him, Hey you, get offa my cloud.

But I jes say, You's only dreamin all that, baby. Don't be scared.

What a they want? What a they tryin t'do? They tryin t'kill me?

Jes stand right up an look close at it.

Then I say, Fuggit, I'm goin for my own.

An here, steppin right inta my dream come a snake. Wrigglin along right belly t'the ground, like waitin for me t'say somethin.

So I say, Hey Mister Snake, you live right down where it's at, tell me somethin. These here peoples we calls the ofay, what's the matter with them?

Snake say, Don't wanna take life like it is, leave it like you finds it. Been tryin t'make it somethin else. Plain forgot what it was in the first place.

Yeah. Well why they wanna fuckover the whole world behind that?

Snake say, Everybody's afraid. Livin in some highass dream an they scared a anybody else not bein in that dream with 'em.

Hey, I'm dreamin this here with you—ain't that right, Mister Snake?

He say, Yeah but you know you is. Ofay's in some nightmare they don't know is a dream.

Yeah, like how much machines an guns an steel this'n'that they got, huh. Makes 'em feel they's better'n other peoples.

Ah, Mister Snake say, but get t'this. If the ofay knowed they jes's hip as anybody, you wouldn't need all that heavy stuff. Same with niggers—you'd come on like you is, steada puttin on all that heavy lipflappin jazz.

Dig it, Mister Snake. Lately I been passin this one corner an hearin a lotta badmouthin this one blackman puttin down, all that Kill Whitie noise. Is yo' hip, Snake? But you know somethin? Go-*dam* I can't believe it. Cause I tricks all kinda mens an I knows it for a stone certain, some blackies is whities on the inside, an some whities is blacker'n a brother. An that there badmouth on the corner, I gots a feelin he some kinda ghosty white inside.

Sure enuff, Mister Snake say. Runnin the ofay game. An you gonna be onta him pretty soon. Lookahere, he only tryin t'put y'all in his bag. Usin his front—black skin. Gonna make it, too, long's peoples is afraid t'look behind the front inta the dark insides. Yonder sittin cross the room from you—that man's afraid t'peek the

152

black dark inside where he's at now. Dig it? Nothin but mohnstahs in his own dark insides—gonna see them mohnstahs every place he look.

You hear that, Jay? I say—like in my mind I say, Quit fightin an take a look at them mohnstahs.

Then I get back with this Mister Snake I'm dreamin up. He's scootin round the floor, like thinkin, waitin on what I'm gonna say next. So I say, Lookahere, if whitie's ofay is the black dark inside his own self, what's all this other ofay that got me so strungout?

Same thing, he say. Everybody's ofay is the black dark inside.

Sho it, I say, Mister Snake you is some kinda jive mothah. *My* ofay ain't no black dark inside *me!* They outside, an don't try t'tell me different.

Your ofay's a nigger. His nigger's an ofay.

Well ain't that a pretzel!

Sure enuff, Snake say. Layin near my feets now, smilin up, like laughin at me. Then he slide on around a bit, an he say, You done let it upset you, momma. Let it get you so ofayed up you's a nigger. It's jes one big two-timin nowhere.

Well it ain't me *made* it that way, Mister Snake. An I don't see no way out.

You done forgot yo' last trip. How you was a healer an all. Remember?

Yeah, that's right. Last trip, I seen myself way back in scenes like outa bible stories.

Snake say, Now let's run one a them scenes again. See here, look at who you was.

An here's me, standin on a beach, an out there in the ocean is boats. Ole fashioned kinda boats with wooden sides an lots a sails. An all of a certain up outa the ocean come mens in steel hats and suits, all glintin in the bright sun, beards stickin out they hats. Yeah, this scene's a pick-up from my last trip. I's wearin the same clothes. Bright colors, oh real bright. But they don't blind the eye like them steel suits.

Mister Snake say, Pay attenshun now. An I see all these steel suits pile up around an point spears at me, like I mean 'em harm. But I don't. I'm only tryin t'ax 'em why they wearin all that steel for. It's hot!

Mister Snake say it fore I ax it, he say, They scared a you powers. Spears is the only kinda mojo they know. That's the nittygritty. Scared a you when they don't have no cause t'be. Fuckinover you bad behind that, an now they gots cause t'be scared—they sickness done spread. But dig it—they all around *you,* but the black dark inside *them,* that's what dominizin the whole scene. Thinks that's you, so they is fuckinover you. Everybody's ofay is the black dark inside, same as everybody's nigger is.

Well shut my mouth!

Mister Snake go wigglin round some more, like dancin. Leave me t'watch how these steel mens take off the clothes I was wearin—a real jazzy hat a feathers, skirt t'match, all wild jumpin colors—an put me in some drab ole gunny sack, think they took away my powers that way.

I say, Hey Mister Snake, the onlyest way for me t'get outa this mess is catch they sickness an turn it back around on 'em. Yeah, what goes out around come back around, huh.

Mister Snake say, She-it, you sound like that street-corner badmouth. Lookahere.

An now I'm at some goins-on that ain't been yet. Here's all them em-efs stranglin in they own steel bombs an stuff. I help 'em take all that steel off, but then steada jes thankin me, they fallin down in front a me an commence t'beg me not t'hurt 'em.

154

I yell, Mister Snake, you quit that. You doin a put-on, makin fun a the way I was beggin the night a the police raid.

No no, he say. Stay with it, look some more.

An here they all is, naked as can be, pilin up around me on the floor, all ackin jes like this one trick I got, takes off his clothes, lays a buggy whip near my hand, and he crybaby an bedevil the hell outa me not t'hurt him. Don't let up till I whump him like he thinks his momma shoulda done.

Mister Snake, you tryin t'tell me I oughta whump all these mothahs?

Say, Take another look, momma.

Well I do, an I swear t'god an allah both, they all turn t'spades that took a milkbath. Yeah, they's white Nee Grows.

An Mister Snake say, See there—you done got to 'em without even tryin. Negrofied 'em. All the time they thunk they was dominizin you down t'the all-blowed-out blues, but you still had soul powers an you was steady negrofyin 'em. Now they wants t'quit dominizin. It's a habit an they wants t'coldturkey but they don't got the soul powers. So you's right back t'start, you's a healer again.

The hell I is! Mister Snake, I don't give a dam for the whole mess of 'em. Give me back my first clothes —that's all I wants from them. You skip right on by all the fuckinover they done for so long. But I remember. Oh yeah! Let 'em pay off now. Yeah, get 'em t'hand me money an plenty of it. Come on. Not one of 'em is offerin me *money*.

Mister Snake say, She-it! Ain't you been a hor long enough t'know about money? What's a matter with you, bitz? Ain't you ever gonna figure it out? Long's them negrofied ofays got you bamboozled on money, an you *needs* the money they is handin out, they dominizin. They don't gotta keep you flatbackin t'make it a dominizin scene. Long's you slippin about lookin for a hand with money in it, the game's the same. Now pay some mind t'this, momma. These negrofied ofays I's showin you here, they ain't handin you no money. You see why?

Yeah! Cause I don't need no money now.

That's where it's goin.

Cause I done took it back, my share a all the stuff they stole with all they guns an legalizin. It all come back around.

That's where it's goin.

Everybody got a share now. Nobody needs money.

Oh you's black as a tack an brighter 'n white.

Sure enuff! But what they after now?

Well look at 'em.

They lookin for me t'dominize 'em back? Ha! Well if it's a whumpin they wants, I'll do it with a feather. She-it, I'll jes put 'em in a hangup an leave 'em.

Figure it out—which nigger's the ofay now?

Ain't this a comedown! Mister Snake, look at them poor souls. All woked up from that dream they was havin, found out it was only a dream. So brung down behind wakin up! You think I ever wanna get brung down like that? Man, I'd rather do a floatout on aitch. Yeah, that dominizin scene's a hype.

Well if you ain't gonna dominize 'em back, what're you gonna do?

Let 'em go. Yes sir, I sure am. Mister Snake, I don't need no hype like that.

Snake smile an wag his head over at Jay Checkerboard.

What're you jookin around for now, Snake?

He say, You gonna cut that dominizin hype loose, what're you doin with him?

156

Lookahere, this man say he gonna *save* me.

Ha! From *what?*

Save me from the ofay by takin me in. Inta the *ofay?* Ha! Yeah, I gotcha, Mister Snake. The ofay's the nigger. Ain't got nowhere t'take me in at. Yeah, an life's movin too fast for that jazz. I see black ofays an white niggers zoomin off t'nowhere faster'n the speed a sound—yak yak yakkin how they's innagratin. But they ain't no difference in 'em—they all tangled up t'gether, so how the hell *can* they innagrate? They all tangled up inside an too busy puttin on fronts.

Mister Snake goes scoochin around thinkin some more, then he say, Now this whiteman's part Nee Grow, same as you. Onlyest difference is the front. Him save you? She-it. Sayin that is jes his way a askin you t'save *him.*

Well tell him t'forget it, I ain't no preacher. Ain't out t'save nobody from nothin. I digs that ole downhome thing—take life like it is, leave it like you find it.

Snake say, She-ee-ee-it! Bob his head back an forth an he say, Get ahold on yo'self, momma. You soundin like the oh-riginal tightass missy ann of all time. You gonna catch that ofay-nigger sickness—or is you gonna use soul power t'heal that ofay-nigger sickness? You know godam right well you's on you choices—you give him that pill. You know he gonna come out some other way'n he went in.

That's *his* problem, how he come out. Lookahere, I's gonna come out some other way too.

You mean you ain't gonna help get the nigger outa the ofay?

Snake, you enough t'make me dance, fart, sit up an bark! Now I don't wanna hear no more about no dark inside a nothin. Lookahere, that man live so deep inside the dominizin ofay, it's a joke t'even talk about it.

157

Lives in the ofay an the ofay lives in him, an that's the ee-fuckin-*end* of it. I can't heal nothin.

Mister Snake catch hold a his tail an turn himself inta a hoop, goes rollin round the room, rollin an laughin.

Quit that rollin an hear what I say, Snake. You ever dig that man talkin? Sound like a tee vee announcer. Got ofay in his blood so bad I'd have t'give him an all-out nigger change-over. An how can I do that?

Snake slither-dance around, laughin some more. Then he say, You is *blockin,* bitz!

Well fuggit! I'm gonna throw that em-ef away like a pair a ole shoes—you know it, too. Soon's Sonny inta somethin new, gonna leave this trick an get on back where I belongs. So quit tryin to make a *thing* out of it.

Who is you tryin t'kid, momma? You blinded by his front same as he is by yours? You got nigger mohnstahs on the dark ofay inside yo'self!

Gonna pick up a stick an knock yo' head off, Snake, you don't quit sassin me. Lookahere, I ain't talkin nigger an ofay no more, I's talkin mans. I don't need no man, no way.

Yeah? What a you gonna do—buy a dildo? She-it, you jes tryin t'slip the pitch.

Ooh Snake, you sure is a bitch! Don't know why I ever dreamed you up. Gonna un-dream you the hell outa here, you don't quit runnin them crazy games.

Shhh, Snake say. Hush up an dig it—he's dreamin *you* up now. See what he dreamin, momma? Him an you is ole folks t'gether, rockin on the back stoop, growed ole an ready for the next life. You gots chillren and they has chilren, an he's happy as a pumpkin.

I don't give a dam what he's dreamin, Snake.

Don't make no nevermind t'you, eh. You's cold-hearted t'the end, eh bitz? You likes it better in the dominizin scene where he's the ofay an you's the nigger —hoein you blackass t'cop his niggerin ofay money, eh?

Gonna take you by the tail an sling you in the ocean, Snake.

Zip unnerneath the sofa, stick his head out an he say, You dum funky woolyhead hoe, you wants that man t'get the ofay out his blood, but you ain't even gonna think about gettin the nigger outa your blood. What a hangup, momma. Look at him—plain t'see he's working out on somethin. Was you took him by the hand an led him inta them woods. You wanna make it out, better let him take you. Stick out you hand—you is all spun around ass backwards an he seein daylight up ahead. Ain't neither one gonna get out that ofay-nigger bag, less you *both* does. Unnerstand? You in it t'gether now. Ain't no gettin out alone. So stick out you hand, momma.

Well that's all I can take a that snake. I chase him outa my dream. Yeah, I disappear him. She-it, I can't *live* with them pitchers he jammin my head with. Life I'm in won't allow it.

Next thing I know, Jay done come over an took me by the hand. Settin here lookin at my hand, turnin it this way an that. Seem like a long time.

Sure is workin out hard on somethin. I could know what it is if I let myself. But ole Mister Snake is right —I been a nigger long's the ofay been the ofay, an I jes don't got noshun number one what else t'be. Caught the black side a the white sickness.

Well he finely turn my hand loose, an then he goes for the door. Out the door an down the steps.

An all of a certain I gots t'get up an go too. Yeah, it's like he's pullin me along.

Down on the beach here's him, dancin with the wind.

Ocean dancin with 'em too—clouds makin the music.

Well I bees a dirty em-ef, that es-oh-bee done cop my trip for a certain. Onlyest thing I can do now is rush down an see can I catch a contack.

Ole Mister Snake was right. Mahstah pill showin Jay some real pretty daylight up ahead.

So I wangles my way up close by his side t'hitchhike a ride on the rest a his trip.

I guess I was still feeling the effects of that pill the next morning when I woke up. Because everything looked so sharp, so colorful and exquisite. Got out of bed and looked out the window and the sea was like a gigantic diamond sparkling in the morning sun.

Then I became aware of someone watching me. I turned and did a double-take straight out of some old fashioned comedy routine. I mean for just an instant I wondered, what's this?—did I leave a part of myself in bed?

And the next instant I remembered, and I asked her, "What was that pill you gave me?" And she told me: LSD.

Wow! If I'd known that yesterday, I'd never have taken it. Not for love nor money. Unless I had a qualified physician around. Isn't LSD a threat to society? Unless properly administered?

Well, I was worrying over this when I noticed that she was watching me with great concern. Enveloping me in this warm concern it seemed, and it gave me an urge to envelop her, to wrap her in my arms and cuddle her. So I got back into bed and did.

She dozed off again, but I lay awake with fireworks of thoughts and impressions going off inside my mind. Everything seemed to have a certain something about it I'd never noticed before. Her hair against my cheek —I turned my head and looked at it closely, and it seemed so lively. A bundle of tiny, tight, springy little curlicues, and it seemed to glow. A wooly ball of blue-black glow. I began inspecting each and every tiny little wiry twig of it, and then I found one of my own hairs lying on the pillow, picked it up with thumb and forefinger and dropped it on her ball of blue-black —and almost laughed out loud at the sight of it.

Then I got caught up marveling at how that glowing blue-black was such a wonderful topping for her face. Suddenly so much seemed so incredible, so absurd. Like, why are there no movie stars with faces like this, topped with such glimmering blue-black? And why does Odessa cover it up with that silly wig?

Brand new—that's how I was feeling. The words "born again" came to mind and they seemed to fit. Because I seemed to be looking out at the world with the same sense of enchantment I remember having at certain moments as a child.

Then I thought of the words "life everlasting" and how many times I've sat in church and snoozed to the sound of some minister rumbling out those words. And checked my watch to see how much longer I'd have to listen to him. Because I really believed that when you die, you die, period. "Life everlasting" were just hocus-pocus words conjured up for church services. But today? Suddenly my whole body is tingling with the clear knowledge of life everlasting—and it has nothing to do with angels perched on clouds playing harps.

What's that line from *Marat/Sade*? Something about death adding to nature's compost heap. Yes, that's what life needs to be everlasting—death. It seemed quite clear to me today. Birth is a form of death and death is a form of birth, and somehow I've always known this, it's just that I didn't want to admit knowing.

Well, at least I'd stored it away in my memory, and now another stored-away memory came parading out to salute. A Quaker I'd once talked to had said that he will have life everlasting through his children, and all the children on earth are his. I thought that was ridiculous nonsense when I heard it, but now I find it perfectly sensible, perfectly correct.

Why have I always resisted such meanings? Were they some kind of threat to me? Was I trained to banish them from my mind? But who—

I was interrupted by the ringing of the phone. Had to dismantle our comfortable entwining of arms and legs to reach over her and pick it up.

"Mr. Holland," shrilled my secretary, "have you forgotten the Saturday emergency meeting of the board? Aren't you coming in today?"

I almost blurted out what I was tempted to say: Miss Quartz, I'm coming very much *in* today, and from a long way *out*.

But I just said, "No."

"Are you sick, Mr. Holland?"

"No."

"Are you sure you're all right?"

And I relished saying, "I'm very much all right today, Miss Quartz, and wish you were the same."

"Well, what shall I tell the board? Shall I tell them you'll *not* be in?

"—Mr. Holland? Are you still on the line?"

No, Miss Quartz, I said silently, for the first time in my life I am *off* the line. And as for the board—well, I was having a vision of the board as a piece of wood. My desk. And I laughed out loud at Miss Quartz addressing my desk.

"The *board*," she persisted, "I've been instructed by the board to inform you that you are requested to— that your presence is requested at this morning's emergency meeting of the board."

Why is her voice so shrill, I wondered. Like a scratchy old record she's forced to keep playing.

I put my head back down on the pillow and listened to her breathing as she waited for me to reply. I closed my eyes and saw her face, and when she shrilled on repeating herself, my old secretary came to mind vividly. A sexy chick, used to wage her own personal war on the Courthouse "fatcats," as she called them. I bought her a tape recorder and she kept it under her bed, and I used to drop in and listen to her sessions with some of those fatcats. They fired her for "insubordination" and assigned Miss Quartz to me. She's fortyish and strives mightily to be as efficient as a machine. A Model-T Ford, tooling along at full throttle, blasting away on her airhorn, like she's doing now.

I hung up. My mind was much too busy this morning to cope with such a silly question as, am I or am I not coming in. As for the board, fuck it with a sixpenny nail. And Miss Quartz, that prune-faced Model-T—if I hadn't hung up I'm sure I'd have said something like, Hey Susie Quartz, come off it. Quit trying to be some self-driven cog in that crazy machine. Leave the office, come on down here to the seashore and see me. Tell me

164

about it—all those hot desires and bloodthirsty hates you're carrying around inside yourself. Come out from behind that prune face and let me pull your girdle off. After all, we're both in this together, this life.

Then I glanced at the face beside me. Dozing again. Now this is a face of many differences, many faces. At the moment it's completely relaxed and pleased with itself. Like a cat in the sunshine. But I've seen it twisted and grimacing with rage, I've seen it long with terror, and I've seen it grinning and twinkling with pure sexual lust. The other night I watched this face regarding her cooking—quick, attentive, sort of playfully serious —and this morning I saw it radiating warm concern like an electric heater.

Now why is it, I wondered, that this girl has such an ever-changing face, so many faces, while Miss Quartz has only that one prune-faced mask of stiff Model-T efficiency? Is that what becomes of a face after so many years of being part of that bureaucratic machine? Miss Quartz has been that for probably twenty of those forty-odd years of hers. Of hers? No, those years weren't even hers—they got swallowed up by the machine.

Poor woman! Whatever caused her to do it? She had her own life to live. How come she never got to it?

But what about *me?* Who do I think *I* am? Who serves that machine more enthusiastically than I do?

Wow! I guess LSD really *is* a threat to society. I mean considering the thoughts I'm having. Like, what is this political machine I'm part of? Harry the Hoop, Herskowitz, Captain Hood, Hook County—what's it all about?

But the phone was ringing again. "I just want to remind you, Buddy boy. Remember our talk the other day? Well, this is no time for you to take a vacation.

Doesn't look good. So come on, pry yourself loose from that black twoit and get on back here with your own kind."

My own kind!

I hung up on Harry and thought about my nephew, my sister's baby. He's part Negro. Yes, he came out revealing to all the world that the Holland family has Negro blood somewhere in its past. My sister's married to a Swede, a *pure* Swede. So the Negro blood comes from our side of that union, which means that I am part Negro. Which means that—who the hell is my own kind? Harry Hooper and the Courthouse fatcats?

And then it hit me, the answer to that other question. This political machine I'm such a smooth-working part of—its purpose is to perpetuate the powerful in power! That's all. It's as simple as that. And what the powerful want is more power. And some of the really grim ones want absolute power. But the really fantastic part of it all is, there are so many people who *want* to be controlled. And I cringed to realize that I am one of them. Or was. A controlled controller. Being controlled by the powerful means security. I mean, financial security.

Well, I'd always known this, it's just that I never wanted to admit that I knew it. But where am I now? If I leave all that behind . . . ?

My God, suddenly there's so much happening. Like Harry, why is he so concerned? Is *he* afraid that I'll quit? That I'll stop supplying myself for the running of his machine? And—most amazing thought!—maybe I will quit.

And a hundred others will rush to grab my job. Serving the powerful's will to power—that's how you make a living. So why should Harry even care if I quit? I mean he'd have a real worry if everybody quit. Harry Hooper the power over the community would become just what he likes to say he is—a *part* of the community. But that's what he really is, in a way. The man with two families—one white, the other black, one born to inherit his power and wealth, the other born powerless, poor.

Come to think of it, that man has a problem.

But the phone was ringing again. "Were we . . ." Harry asked cautiously, "cut off?"

He'd feel relieved if I'd lie and say, yes we were cut off. But I said, "No, I hung up on you, Harry."

And I listened to his breathing whistling through the wires. And visualized how he must look with those emotions churning in him.

Then, very calmly, he said, "What's *wrong* with you, Buddy boy?"

Well, then I let go—covered the phone's mouthpiece and lay back on the pillow and roared.

"*Say* something!"

And I couldn't resist. I said, "Harry, what's wrong with me is, I've been trying to figure it out. I mean, what do you *want?* What do you *really* want? With me, with anybody. Do *you* know?"

And I hung on, hearing his breathing.

"Well well well," he said finally, "I sure am disappointed in you. Sounds like that nigger has you in her clutches. Never thought I'd see the day my boy J. C. would let this happen to himself. You're *dead,* Buddy boy. Ruined! If you don't throw that nigger out of there and come on back here with your friends. . . ." Then his tone changed: "You sure do have everybody worried. Your loving wife, all your good friends. Now you *know* a man in his right mind just doesn't do the things you're doing and we'd all feel a whole lot better if you'd come back and let your friends *help* you."

"What are you afraid of, Harry?"

"Me? Afraid? What are you talking about? I just hate to see this *happen* to you."

"See *what* happen?"

"Well, it's nothing we can't straighten out in time, Buddy boy. And there's no use making it any worse by wasting another minute. Hop in your car and come back to the fold."

"Can't do that, Harry. Intercourse with sheep is ill . . . legal."

Which caused Odessa to let out a short "Ha!" and pull the covers over her head.

"Is that your message to the board this morning?"

"The board? Oh, tell the board I'm chagrined. That's the word—*sha-grinned*. Tell them I'm chagrined and am no longer *with* them."

"Are you trying to tell me you're *resigning?*"

"Resigning? Well, no, not exactly. I'm re-*sign*ing. I'm—"

"You're *sick*," he shouted.

"No! I'm well! Or at least I'm healing. I'm recovering, rejoining. Re-*sign*ing and rejoicing."

"Or else you're drunk—sick or drunk!"

"I'm as sober as a . . . as a *stone*."

"Buddy boy, you're out of your mind."

"Yes, that's it! I'm out of my mind—the mind that was mine yesterday. And I'm . . ."

But where am I today?

I hung up on him again. And it felt like dropping a curtain between where I was yesterday and wherever I am today. But figuring out where I am today—that's the most important thing in my life.

My life. Yes, that's it—the most important thing in my life is my life. My life *is* life. And maybe—can it be possible?—by dropping a curtain on Harry and all that, maybe I'll raise a curtain on my life. *My* life.

168

My *job?* Who needs it! It's just a clown show for egos. A game of king of the hill. A silly boondoggle, a treadmill. A going-nowhere ratrace—on a gloriously advanced technological treadmill. And if you stay on for the duration you get to retire in decrepitude in Florida.

Put out a press release now and then, keep everybody properly confused. Put together speeches for the members of the inner circle. I have six standard formats, all hot air. Yank one out, change some words here and there, dictate it into Miss Quartz, and out comes a new speech. Always says the same thing: Give me your money for my campaign so I can flood the public mind with advertisements for myself, and I'll see that you make more money later. Invest in me, for I am devoted to getting money out of the taxpayers and into your pockets.

Then from under the covers, Odessa said, "Are you still tripping? Cut it loose, let's have some fun."

Fun! Ah yes! Who needs retirement in decrepitude when you can retire under the covers. It's just as warm as Florida.

But the phone rang again. She stuck her head out and said, "Ain't they never going to leave you alone?" And mumbled something about how this place sounds like a two-bit whorehouse, with that phone ringing all the time.

Well, I was resisting the temptation to find out who it was this time, when I became aware of sand in the bed. Like itchy little ballbearings between me and the sheet, and I said, "What's all this *sand* doing in bed?"

"You brung it in from rolling on the beach. Yesterday —don't you remember?"

Oh yes, now I remember. Those grains, those statements of joy. Yesterday, but today they're just . . . itchy sand and they don't belong in bed.

Don't know how many times the phone rang before I gave up resisting and grabbed it. Barbara—in top form. Like she was sucking a lemon, she said, "If you ever want to see your son again"—or like she's a bitter-sweet pitchwoman for the welcome wagon—"you'll get that black nigger bitch out of there. And if she isn't out of there by noon today, Mister, I'm going to have all the locks changed. And I'm going to file for divorce on Monday. Do you hear me?"

"Things are moving right along," I said.

"Well, that's just the beginning, Mister. Because *you* —are in *trouble*—up to your *neck!*"

"You'll have to tell me all about it sometime," I said, "but right now, I'm too busy to listen." And I hung up.

Then, for just a moment, I felt very sad about it. I mean, I wondered, what will she do without me? How will the poor girl get on in life?

But I was fooling myself with a phoney worry. What she'll do without me is marry another me. Another one who is what I was. And she'll beat on him with her bitterness, which will be much better all the way around, because what I am now just doesn't go with what she is.

I mean I can't help it that she was seduced as a teen-ager, and it's gotten to the point where I couldn't care less. Never did understand it. How could the guy be a *child molester?* She was *seduced*—at age *fourteen*. And is it *my* fault she got traumatized by the legal battle that followed? She squealed on him and her parents had them throw the book at him, and he's still in jail, the guy that did it. Sometimes I wish he'd get out of jail and spank her bare behind. Hard. For *both* of us. Then she could spend the next year or so telling her psychoanalyst about *that*.

Wow! To think that only yesterday I believed it was

me who was in trouble. What a laugh. It's Barbara and that crowd who are in trouble. I've just arrived in a state of *un*trouble. I'll be damned if I'll go back to their state of trouble—and she'd better not come down here and bust in on us.

But maybe I should go back—as the Courthouse jester. I could walk around speaking my mind. "Hi there, Harry Hooper, and how are your black selves today?" And when I catch G. W. Jones serenading Harry with one of his back room renditions of "Mammy," I could say, "Go wash that black paint off your face, Mr. Jones. What do you think this is, a minstrel show?"

Well, that role tempts me. But could the jester-me survive that grim Courthouse atmosphere? Or would I burn up upon re-entry?

Besides, right this minute Harry's probably pow-wowing with the board about what I said over the phone. So the hell with it. I've got too many thoughts to parade out and interrogate.

No, that's not quite it. What's really happening to me is that today I can ask questions I didn't allow myself to ask yesterday. And some of the answers are self-evident.

Like the question, Should I go back to my job at the Courthouse? Answer: No, because I am no longer *with* them. Question: But if I'm not with *them*, where am I? Answer: That's a good question. But at least I can look back, now, and see what I was. I'm not afraid of it any more. Wow, what a wall of verbal garbage I was putting up to keep from knowing what my job was really all about.

Well, that's not quite true. Because I really did know —it's just that I couldn't *admit* knowing. So I hid knowing behind a tremendous pile of lies and half-truths. That's what my life was, lies and half-truths.

171

And today, here I am sort of uprooted from that pile of lies and half-truths, and it's a bit scary—drifting away with nothing to hang onto. I've got to find something to hang on to.

Like what? It may take time to figure that out. Maybe I'll sell some real estate and take off a year or so. Just goof off, look back at what I was a part of. Analyze it, discover exactly what it really is.

And with that thought in mind I postponed all other questions and ordered them to stop pushing and shoving for a hearing in my mind. Because Odessa's lips and fingers were asking me a question—about what spectacular sensations a day like today might begin with.

And to think of all the days I wanted to begin like this! Instead of forcing myself out of bed, to waste myself in the intoxications of the busy Courthouse treadmill.

I reached under the covers and slid my arms around her, savoring the feel of it, the touch of our skins, enjoying every tiny nuance. Two bodies touching. How simple and beautiful. And profound. Her dark body and my light one. Night and day, the two halves of the earth in orbit. Now there's time and space for us to accept this, now that I've stopped striving to play the successful young cog in the power machine, there is time to play with these thrills and really dig the sweetness of moments like this.

And when the phone rang the next time, I picked it out of its cradle and pulled it under the covers and tucked it between our four legs. Whoever was calling —that's all I had to say to him.

Sittin in the livinroom, sippin coffee, wonderin how's the best way t'go after my money.

Gonna leave. Soon's Zeek gets here. Yeah, put in a call t'the Paradize this mornin whilest Jay was in the baffroom. Found out my ole man trying t'coldturkey. Tole Zeek, Get on down here an carry me back.

Jay ain't had much t'say this mornin. Busy in his head. That an bein on the phone. So I ain't tole him I'm leavin.

Well all of a certain he wanna talk now. Say, Remember three year ago? That thing we had with Herman Pennypacker?

Yeah, I was unnerneath this big politico, weigh three hunner pounds. Was tryin t'trick with him, but steada comin he went. Died on me. All three hunner pounds.

Jay say, I put up such a smokescreen a lies about that, maybe I never will know the truth a what hap-

173

pened. Wow what a liar I been. Gag zoots! Buildin a wall a slogans tween me and the truth.

Ole Mahstah pill knock a hole in that wall, baby?

Yep. T'day I'm a brand new man!

Puts down some coffee an he say, That place you was livin then. The eye double aye double pee—wasn't that a commie way t'live?

Hell no! Was only a common sense way. All we done was live goin the other way from the ofay. Share an share alike. Shared the money an we shared the work. Onlyest things we didn't share was our own personel stuff.

He say, I really don't see how that's such a threat. Wonder why that scares people?

Humph! Pill musta took him through some funny changes, huh.

I say, I don't know. Maybe them squares is scared everybody get t'livin like we was, an then who'd they have left t'dominize? Machines? Ain't no fun dominizin machines.

I wonder, he say, is that possible?

Everybody jes copout? Sure! Leave all them Charlies up there top they big piles a money, everybody else start in all over again and pretty soon we all be up top a pile a million times bigger'n what they gots now. Be so much cash nobody'd need it. Be like air.

He say, Wonder how many people think that way?

Don't worry, most folks gets car-driving mixed up with thinkin. Only thinks where they's allowed to. Don't let they thinkin run no redlights, an Big Charlie done set up them redlights so's most people never give this bizness no thought a-tall. Me, I goes by them redlights when I'm drivin, but not when I'm thinkin. Ain't gonna allow the ofay t'run my thinkin down thruways an one-way streets, deadends an stop signs an such. No,

an I don't allow the ofay t'stick words in my mouth
neither. I talks the downpeoples talk. Can say it like I
feels it in downpeoples talk. Slip inta highass white talk
an I gets t'soundin like some strivin pride tee vee thing.
Yeah, an nobody in life can mean t'say what some a
them mothahfuggahs come out with. You ever lissen to
'em? I mean *hear* what they be sayin? Man, sometimes
I lay up in my room by myself an I tripout on them tee
vee strivin prides—so spooked they's tumblin out words
t'mean somethin *else*.

Hey lookahere, one part a my trip I dream them tee
vee 'nouncers all of a certain gots t'what they bosses
been pushin 'em at. Come on an they say, Okay everybody—all you niggers an all you whitetrash too, we
gonna take you off an get rid a ya now, cause we's sick
an tired a keepin y'all alive on welfare when we ain't
got nary a need for ya. Not no more. Machines does
the work for less. We gonna get rid a y'all an have a lot
more money for ourselves.

Oh *no*, Odessa. That could never happen in the you-
es-aye. That's jenoside, killin off people like that. Meri-
cans don't *do* that.

Liked t'choke on my coffee. Got a mind t'ax this fool
when he see 'em *not* doin like that. Man, killin's they
main thing.

But fuggit, I don't. I jump ahead an I say, Well lissen
heah, I gots another scene. Shuckin The Man. Everybody rised up t'gether, tellin him, Get t'steppin—take
all them guns an planes an bombs, an gather up all you
james bond honky Hunkies an move on outa here.
Yeah, an that's the day I square up—I ever live t'see it.
Place fulla house apes an a man out doin his thing.

That's *it*, Odessa. He gladeyes all over me an he say,
That's jes what we *are* going to *do!*

Baby, you must think you some kinda hen's ass. You

175

gonna put me an you wife in here *both?* What country you think you livin in? Don't you got it straight yet? You's in one race an I's in another, an we sure ain't runnin in the same direckshun. Ain't never gonna catch *me* runnin with the white race, neither. Them packrats goin straight t'nowhere faster'n the speed a sound. An they don't allow nobody the color a you t'cross over t'my side. So you jes turn that trippin loose—movin me in here.

Ah, he say, but that's no good, keepin the races separate.

Yeah? Well Big Charlie knows what he doin. Fixin t'innagrate the black an white an make some *new* kinda separates. But he *gots* t'have separates t'stay on top.

Here's him, he's scrunchin up his face an lookin all fulla pain, an he say, I don't *believe* in separatin the races. Not any more.

What the fug's believe got t'do with it? I'm sayin how it *is.*

Odessa, please, let's give it a try. We can make it t'gether.

Pill still got you, baby. Us make it t'gether? Ha! What kinda powers you gonna use agin that white magic? Black magic? Sweetheart, you funny as a crutch. Onlyest way you ever live is way up here top side the dollah. You ever poke you haid outside all this white magic? You ever take a look at all them peoples down on the unnerside holdin that dollah up? Hell no! Like all this land you owns. What you gonna *do* with it? What good's it do you, out here all alone, no people t'live on it?

I'm gonna *sell* this land an I'm gonna—

Gonna make a bundle a money, huh.

Sure.

An then what you gonna do?

176

Invest that money, make more money. Keep it workin for me.

Steada you workin, you money's workin.

That's right.

Well ain't that cool! You gets richer an the poor gets poorer, workin for that money that's workin t'make more money.

Jobs, he say, investin *money's* what provide jobs.

Workin t'make you money make you more money? What for? What a you want from all that money? She-it, you whitefolks steady grabbin at green paper an never groovin with what you already has in the first place.

Oh I agree! An I'm gonna find out what I really want.

Well that's *your* hussle, baby, makin more money. My hussle's makin you less money an more happy, an that reminds me, I—

Odessa, be practickle! Say you'll live with me! I'll get a divorce! I'll—

Whoa, slow down!

No, don't slow me down. Love, that's all that matters. Love. I'm so fulla love.

Well I sure do hates t'throw cold water on that love thing, but get t'this. Trick that turn me onta this el-es-dee, he steady yammerin out love love love. Loves the whole world, what he say. But you oughta see him— what he say ain't what he do. Lookahere, how's he gonna walk down the street all fulla nothin but love without getting beat for his change or busted by the fuzz? Stays inside his own pad most a the time. An when he do goes out, he sticks tight close with his asid friends. Loves the jumpin shitfits out the whole world —*at arm's length!*

Take me t'meet him, innerduce us.

Oh baby, turn it loose. Them asidheads so fulla love they can't hardly make it.

But that's jes how *I* feel. Money?—who needs it? Love is all.

Baby, the flip side a love is *hate!* You think the whole world gonna turn over an play on nothin but *love?* From now on? Jes cause you *wants* it to? Try fuckin some cop in the ear with nothin but love. *Luv* you over the head with his billy! Big Charlie ain't got them little chollies out there lissenin for love, an they ain't gonna hear what they ain't sent out t'lissen for. Man, you can't run *your* thing on the fuzz, you gots t'tune in on *his,* an that takes practice. I can do it—I's a hoe, that's my *main* thing, readin minds.

Oh no, he say, not any more. You're all done hoein.

Ooh-wee! Gonna make me a made, eh. Gonna put me in some room readin beds and sheets an pillas, huh. Oh no, baby, no. I'd a lot sooner go round readin mens' minds, trickin an trippin t'the pitchers in they heads. Gonna stay right with mussin beds, let somebody else make 'em.

But . . . don't you wanna get edjukated an do somethin *use*ful?

Useful! Now ain't that a bitch? Lissen heah, I know a girl, she's a typewriter—goes t'some office every day, clickedy-clacks away. Tole me I oughta do somethin *use*ful like that. Give up hoein an get edjukated an be a typewriter all day. That dum broad, I gots more edjukashun climbin in an outa beds'n she ever gonna get fuggin a typewriter. An useful? She-it! Lookahere, I could take her to a coke party, dab a whiff on her pearl-tongue, have one a them hozes t'put his High Johnny-root on her, and she'd sure enuff come away with her ass useful for somethin 'sides fuck with a typewriter all day. An don't say no, I seen it happen.

Okay, okay, you don't wanna be a made an you don't wanna be an office girl. What do you wanna *be?*

Baby, I bees jes what I is—a hoe. That's the jungle they got me livin in. Lotta squares look down on it but I can't help that. I ain't nothin but a hoe an that's all I gots t'be. I could come out that jungle an be a suburb housewife an my own self *both,* I might try it. But on the choices I got, I takes hoein. Yeah, I see them square hypocrits all the time, I know what they's into. Too many of 'em come t'my jungle jes beggin t'get fooled. Payin for some lowdown funky foolery. An them square broads they leave behind, they's talkin one thing, cravin another. Holyrollerin up church aisles an tightass pee-tee-aye sittin, brighteyein preachers an shakin ass in front a bosses. Missy ann chicks out prowlin shoppin centers, all wearin man-catchin clothes an struttin like a pileup a holes when the heat's on. Now you can't tell me them bitzes got they minds all on store buyin. I lissen inta they mens' bedtalk. Tee vee advertizin steady tellin 'em how *hoppy* they gonna be with new this an new that, an they bustin ass tryin t'believe it. In stores peepin this an feelin up that. She-it, they only foolin themselves. Needs body excitement. That's why they stirrin up all that hootin an hollerin an devil noise —barkin Commonism, droppin Compoz, spittin slant talk. Man, ain't nobody gonna make a cooped-up square outa me. With no way t'get after what my body cravin, an get it when she cravin it. Movin round some big ole shoppin center fulla hot twoits an cravin cocks— baby I'd jes have t'rise up an turn on a party. Or go t'jail tryin, one.

Then all of a certain—*beep beep!* Car horn. Look out the winda an there's Zeek.

Jay jump up, say, What's that?

Crab my purse an head for the door.

He say, Where *you* goin?

Leavin.

Whata you mean, leavin?

Be back in a day or two. Got bizness in town. Look over my stuff while I'm gone, okay?

Odessa, you can't leave me now. We got too much t'talk about. Odessa, don't go. I need you. Odessa, stop! Come back here. You can't *do* this t'me. All my life was yestiday. That's all over. Finished, done. Odessa, you got t'help me. *You* gave me that pill!

But I'm down them steps, in that car, tellin Zeek t'go. Roll down the car winda while we pullin out an I holler up, I'm comin back in a day or two, Checkerboard. Seedja later.

Here's him, standin up on the top step lookin stone sure enuff *lost.*

Fuggit. *I* ain't his woman.

Zeek say, What you put on that man?

Everythin I could think of.

You sure done it right.

Course I done it right. Left him with a head fulla black-black pussy.

How much?

Oh! Ooh! Go-*dam,* Zeek. That's the onlyest thing I didn't do right. Forgot t'get my money!

But don't turn back. Lissen heah, I'm gonna get after that man again in a couple days, soon's we got Son off his habit an I'm gonna get my money on the next go-round.

Well Zeek laugh so hard he dam near crack up his car. An back at the Paradize he tells it around that I runned such powerful games on that seashore dude I catched myself up in 'em.

Yeah, an I can't call him a liar, that's the worst part.

Not till I finds out, did that em-ef *mean* what he say? Did ole Mahstah pill really take him through such big-big changes he can't never go back t'what he *was?* An is I jes flatout the dummest broad in the jungle?—fightin so hard a-gin that dream I had with Mister Snake?

They expected me to put up a battle when they came to get me, and I was so startled by them that I did. So they declared me a violent case and brought me here in a straitjacket. It was a pretty amazing experience.

My wife signed the papers so they could do it. Then she and my former friends at the Courthouse informed the local press, and the headline read, "County Official Is LSD Victim." Now all my earthly possessions are with my wife and her lawyer, pending our divorce.

Well, I was pretty shook up about it for awhile. But that was several weeks ago. Since then I've quieted down. Don't have time to be angry or upset any more. I'm too busy reading, questioning, learning.

No doubt my old cohorts are saying that I'm out of touch with "reality," and from their point of view, I am. I've quit their "reality"—for ever. And not because of the LSD—not entirely. All my psychedelic trip did for me was tear down some mental blocks, open my mind, fill me with questions. It's the questions themselves that have made me a dropout from their "reality."

Like, why is it that in this fabulously wealthy land of ours some of us are born with too much and others are born completely dispossessed? And what is this "law and order" that is trying to keep it this way? Isn't there more than enough to go around? Why this life-wrecking ratrace? And if we do have to make some kind of race out of life, why can't we all get off to an even start? Isn't that what a government is for—to provide equal opportunity?

Just a few of the questions I've been pondering—and talking over with a couple of other inmates here, a former psychiatrist and a former Communist revolutionary. They're dropouts from their former "realities" too. Three souls in search of a new reality, that's us.

George, the former Commie, and I share a joke now and then about how the chief psychiatrist here keeps telling us to "forget politics!" Well, for awhile we both tried. But then it dawned on us that politics is as much a part of human life as food is. So now, instead of trying to forget our old politics, we are remembering them. And the rivers of blood that have flowed in their names.

The really ironic thing about all that is, most of our disagreement is merely words. Sounds. Because when you get right down to cases, the kind of society he wants isn't much different than the kind I want. And the more we talk about our politics, the clearer this becomes.

Odessa sat in on our discussion last Monday. She visits every Monday as regular as the earth turns, and listening to her has made me realize how dis-educated I've been. She's never been near a classroom in her life, yet when someone comes up with some heavy political or philosophical concept, all he has to do to get her to grasp it is say it in language she understands.

Strange, how I used to think of her language as vulgar, unrefined, loaded with "dirty" words. It's the version of the American language that I was trained to use —that's what's really dirty, truly obscene. The correct grammar and euphemisms of the liar, the thief, the killer.

I've been listening in to her language lately and I'm constantly surprised by how rich it is. And how easily it bends and adapts so she can make it say what she wants to say. It's given me one more reason to be glad I'm not "pure" white. Glad I'm part Negro, part Afro-American, part non-white, whatever you want to call it. I can no longer see things in simple terms of skin color or "race."

Like that race riot we had locally. Pardon me, I mean the police raid. Anyhow, we were talking about it last Monday, because we go on having these major and minor explosions in hundreds of other towns across the country. We've had Black Power advocates saying if America don't come around we'll burn it down. We've had white racists saying that if Negroes don't quiet down we'll exterminate them. We've had TV commentators saying things like, "Our house is on fire— we've got to put out the flames." We've had Hubert Humphrey saying we need a Marshall Plan for American cities, and we've had Lyndon Johnson saying go to church and pray.

And none of those clowns in City Hall or Washington ever stops to think about what *made* the poor in the first place, it seems. I mean, what created this tremendous gulf between the dispossessed and the rest of our society?

Well, last Monday I was listening to Odessa tell about it from her situation in these disunited states and it occurred to me that . . . well, now I know what it is I must do with my life. I know what I have got to do, what my life is for. I'm not sure how I'll go about it, but later for the how. The how will come to me once I get to work on the what.

As I was walking her to the bus stop I said, "You know, Odessa, when you consider what I have and what you have, what I am and what you are, what I lack and what you lack, we have just got to put ourselves together. That way we'll both be so much richer, in so many different ways."

She didn't give me a chance to elaborate. She said, "Man, when are you going to turn that cornball hangup *loose? We* ain't going to put ourselves together—not *here*, in the U. S. A."

"Oh yes we *is*," I said without a moment's hesitation. "The U. S. A. is our home. Now if our home doesn't suit us, we'll just have to tear it down and put it back together again, and this time we'll *make* it suit us. We'll make it suit *us!*"

More'n a week gone by, time Sonny got his habit sweated out. An when I put in a call t'Jay's place, nobody's there. Drived down t'check it out an find the place's locked up tight.

Ooh, Momma! What a second-class fool he made outa you.

Then one night I met up with a sister, she's a addin machine in the cordhouse, an I ax her. She say they tooked him away for a crazy! Showed me where they put it in the papers that the el-es-dee done it. Throwed his ass in a loonybin, called him in sane.

Well I got the number a that place an I kep callin till I got t'talk with him. Tole him right off, Man you owes me a bundle for that time I was with you. When you gonna pay up?

Mothahfuggah lies like a rug, most likely. Tole it that his wife got all his money and he ain't got nothin. An he ax me to run up an see him on Monday.

186

Well I did. What the hell I got t'lose?

Ain't no regular loonybin they keepin him in. No lectrick shock, no goons, none a that mind-smashin shit. This place all grass and trees, statchews an nice lookin thingamajigs. An each crazy got a room like a downtown motel.

Took me up t'his room, lays me like we been doin it for nine long years. Tole him, Baby you sure is a better man in sane than out.

Then I comed back the nex Monday an I spose I'm gonna make it out there *nex* Monday. We been havin some pretty good weekends—ain't nothin doin on Mondays anyhow.

Hey, an I sure been pickin up on stuff, too. We got t'talkin an he tole me t'watch out for this certain-certain streetcorner badmouth, same one I figured for a phoney. Tole me this cat's in the pay a the cordhouse ofay.

Took that back t'the Paradize, got a couple brothers t'go peep that badmouth. An sure enuff, he some kinda two-way hype. He's a *plant*—you dig it? Out on the streetcorner nine o'clock of a Saterdy night rebel rousin, yellin Kill Whitie, Kill Whitie! Up t'his ears in pink pussy two hours later while them peoples he done stirred up is givin themselves t'the police. I mean he's badmouthin like he learned it on his momma's knee an two hours later he wheelin round the suburbs with some seditty blue eye in her nacheral daddy's big black caddy sheen.

Ain't that a bitch! Jive pipeline konkaleen, helpin the polices stir peoples up so's they can't stick t'gether an help each other a-gin them bloodsuckin honkies.

Well he ain't doin it no more. No, cause last Saterdy night when he come out t'shout, he got some shoutin back. I yelled at him myself. Tole him, You jes shut yo' big mouth—go on over with you pink pussycat, see can you kill the whitie in her. Yeah, sock it to her, fill 'er up with Black Power.

He ain't been back since. Good thing, cause we sure do gots trouble aplenty now. Don't need him helpin the whiteman stir up more.

Talk a lotta high-soundin jibberjabber—me an Jay an these two other cats. They thunk I was too dum t'pick up on that talk. Well I tole 'em, y'all really got somethin t'say, run it on down front. Don't jes flap yo' lips an make fancy wind, say it straight out. I may be the dummest broad in the jungle—*my* jungle—but that don't mean y'all gotta make some big mystry outa yours.

An I got 'em doin it, too. We was talkin riot an one a them ax me, Is you against the people *own* stuff in this country?

Hell no, I tole 'em. I ain't a-gin no people that *owns.* I'm a-gin them cuttin out the people that *don't* owns. How come everybody don't own a piece up front? Steada poor peoples workin for the rich folks all the time.

People still gonna fight, he say.

Well, that's cool. Good for the blood—when you fightin one t'one. Onlyest time I don't dig fightin is when some Charlie got you in some army killin an dyin for some kinda devils he carryin round inside his own self. Fuggit, why get killed for some Charlie devil like Commonism? Leave him t'jackoff on that one by his own self.

Yeah, an I showed 'em where it weren't no race riot we done had in this town. Was a mothahfuggin police raid, and we's dam sick'n tired a *them.*

Jay say, That's why no stores got looted, huh.

I tole 'em, Far as store lootin goes, if you was poor, you'd get the sweat looted outa you on a job, you'd get what you got comin looted outa you on short pay, and you'd get need t'buy looted outa you on jip prices an trickanomics. So when you turn it around and loot some store, you only bringin whitie's thing back home to him.

Well Jay say, How can we stop it? Give more t'the poor?

Give! How can The Man give what ain't really his? All Big Charlie can do is share. Share what all the forefathers had a hand in makin. An lookahere, if he don't soon turn it loose, he gonna get it loot-loosened from him. Cause it ain't his t'begin with.

Share, 'eh. Mmm.

Yeah! An quit tryin t'beat life down. Man, sometimes the whole white race look t'me like some big toe tryin t'dominize the rest a the body, tryin t'cause it t'stumble an fall in a fire. But it ain't gonna. An pretty soon, gonna be ole white eye's time t'catch all the hell he done sent out.

When you get outa here, come on over an stay with me awhile, dig it from my side.

Rappin all afternoon like that. Come time for me t'go an Jay's walkin me t'the bus stop, here he come on with some speechafyin. He say, Odessa, me an you got t'put ourselfs t'gether. That way we bees richer.

Well I know he steady gettin more an more turned around on The Man and all he tryin t'do is tell me where he's at now. Didn't mean t'sound cross with him, but I *know* where he's at. Know I'm part a the game t'put him there, cause we all jes part a the game life's playin with us.

But I swear t'god and allah both, I done heard so much pretty talk outa so many white eyes, I jes ain't up t'hearin one more word. Tole him t'shut his big mouth fore it land him in jail—don't talk it, *do* it.

Then I got on the bus an waved him a kiss through the winda, an I had a strong feelin come risin up. He looked a whole lot better'n he ever looked before, standin there. Had an urge t'wrench open that winda an holler out the bus, You already two, three hunner years *late*, mothahfuggah. You ever gonna do it, you better come out that place an get t'steppin. Like that el-es-dee trip—I'll take you by the hand an bring you inta my jungle—side a town I live in—an see can we find us all a way out. You help me outa mines, I'll help you outa yours. We finds the outs an get t'steppin, nothin in life'll stop us, no way.

Well I couldn't get the winda open, but I think he heard me anyhow.

Author's After Words

Back in 1959 when I began what has become this trilogy (*One Hundred Dollar Misunderstanding, Here Goes Kitten, J C Saves*) I had no preconceived idea where these two characters would lead me, their author. During the nine years since, I have undergone some changes and so have they. Their changes are indicated by variations of mood and dialect, mine by what I have imagined them being as they became. I call myself their author, yet I do not really feel I have "created" them. Rather, they found me and in some curious and subtle way I have since followed them.

It's been a trip full of delights, disappointments, surprising turns. Being figments of my imagination, they are aspects of what I am, and of what my society is. For some years I felt they were revealing some horrible premonition, and like a player whose Tarot cards are predicting tragedy, I felt cheated by fate before the event.

Now, looking back on this whole odyssey of changes, where these two characters have led me isn't as horrible as I feared it would be. It even holds out a hint that, after we complete the destruction of what America has been, there will be hope for us to become a society of human beings.